hidden talen

Bello is a digital-only imprint of Pan Macmillan,
established to breathe new life into previously published,
classic books.

At Bello we believe in the timeless power of the imagination,
of a good story, narrative and entertainment, and we want to
use digital technology to ensure that many more readers
can enjoy these books into the future.

We publish in ebook and print-on-demand formats
to bring these wonderful books to new audiences.

www.panmacmillan.co.uk/bello

BELL◎

Richmal Crompton

Richmal Crompton (1890–1969) is best known for her thirty-eight books featuring William Brown, which were published between 1922 and 1970. Born in Lancashire, Crompton won a scholarship to Royal Holloway in London, where she trained as a schoolteacher, graduating in 1914, before turning to writing full-time. Alongside the *William* novels, Crompton wrote forty-one novels for adults, as well as nine collections of short stories.

Richmal Crompton

PORTRAIT OF
A FAMILY

BELL◎

First published 1932 by Macmillan

This edition published 2015 by Bello
an imprint of Pan Macmillan
20 New Wharf Road, London N1 9RR
Basingstoke and Oxford
Associated companies throughout the world

www.panmacmillan.co.uk/bello

ISBN 978-1-5098-1030-7 EPUB
ISBN 978-1-5098-1028-4 HB
ISBN 978-1-5098-1029-1 PB

Typeset by Ellipsis Digital Limited, Glasgow

Visit **www.panmacmillan.com** to read more about all our books
and to buy them. You will also find features, author interviews and
news of any author events, and you can sign up for e-newsletters
so that you're always first to hear about our new releases.

Chapter One

CHRISTOPHER MAINWARING leant back in the corner of his railway carriage and gazed unseeingly at the kaleidoscope of woodland, meadow, town, and village that flashed by. He was a tall spare man of about sixty, with a thin delicately modelled face, mobile lips, hollowed temples, and kind dreamy eyes. It would have been difficult to say in what feature—if in any—lay the hint of weakness that the face undoubtedly conveyed. There was, moreover, a look of strain upon it now, a suggestion of suffering, and, beneath the suffering, fear. His neat grey suit was well brushed and well pressed, the edge of a silk handkerchief showed above the breast pocket, there came from him a faint perfume of eau-de-Cologne, but it was obvious that the care he had given to his toilet was mechanical, the result of the habits of a life-time rather than a token of any present interest in his appearance. His eyes, despite their dreaminess, were bright and restless, and he was obviously unaware of everything around him—the railway carriage, the kaleidoscopic landscape, his fellow-passengers.

He took out his watch with a quick nervous movement. Only a quarter of an hour now. . . . He wondered if anyone would be at the station to meet him. He hoped not. . . . He had written to the children to tell them not to come. In any case, of course, Derek and Frank would be at their work, and Joy would be busy with her children. It was Saturday, so perhaps they would come to see him this evening. Susan had made a ceremonial rite of the Saturday evening family assembly. Nothing had ever been allowed to interfere with it. She had loved to have the "children" about her—Derek and his wife Olivia, Frank and his wife Rachel, Joy and her husband

Bruce. On the whole, he hoped that they would not come to see him this evening. It would be too painful for all of them.

The last time they had met, Susan had been there,—childishly pleased as ever to welcome them, radiantly pretty despite her fifty-five years. Then again he changed his mind and hoped that they would come. The thought of the lonely house filled him with strange panic and set his heart racing in his thin breast.

They had all written to him regularly while he was away—dutiful, bright, little letters, letters that carefully avoided any mention of Susan, and that were too obviously meant to cheer him up. Lethbridge had written also. Perhaps Lethbridge would be at the station to meet him.

For no particular reason he took out his pocketbook and looked at the date. September 15th. . . . Just a month since that garden-party at the Rectory. He remembered standing on the edge of the lawn and watching Susan, who was the centre of a little group beneath the cedar tree. Their eyes had met suddenly, and hers had smiled—an intimate smile, amused, tender, half mischievous, as if she both enjoyed this popularity of hers, and laughed at it, as if only he really understood. He had been married to her for thirty years, but that look had thrilled him as if he were a boy.

His thoughts went back over their married life. It had been unclouded by a single quarrel or even misunderstanding. They had not been as intimate as married people generally are, perhaps. There had always been something elusive and withdrawn about Susan. It had been her greatest charm to him. And he, on his side, had been a romantic, idealising every situation, so that he preferred to worship her on his knees at a distance.

The moments when they drew together in passion had been precious to him, but they had meant less than the normal relations that existed between them—his worship and the veil of glamour and romance that had hung about her in his eyes ever since his first meeting with her. Even after she had borne three children, she had seemed to him in her essence virginal and untouched. Yet she had loved her children, pouring out over them a gay and radiant tenderness that secretly he marvelled at. Motherhood had seemed natural to her, as fatherhood had never seemed natural to Christopher.

His thoughts returned to the garden-party at the Rectory. She had coughed a little that night, and he had listened to her uneasily. The next day he had called in Lethbridge, who diagnosed a slight congestion of one lung. Within a week she was dead.

The day after the funeral Lethbridge had said to him:

"Look here, old man, you've got to get right away for a change at once, or I won't be responsible for the consequences."

He had protested, but Lethbridge had waved aside his protests.

"I understand. I've been through it, though I had a bit more warning than you had. When you look forward now you see your life as a damned stretch of day after day without her, and you feel that you can't go on. Well, you've got to get away from it all,—the house and everything that reminds you of her—and when you come back things won't seem quite so bad. You've not been sleeping, have you?"

"No."

"You're thinking of her all the time?"

"Yes."

"You look ten years older than you did this time last week. You're not really strong, you know. Making a wreck of yourself won't bring her back. You're thinking of her continually. You're going over every minute of your married life with her. You've not slept a wink since she died. Well, you're a doctor, and a better one than I am, and you know where that sort of thing ends. You've got to take yourself in hand."

After Lethbridge had gone, Christopher had felt a sudden impulse to laugh. It was so funny that Lethbridge should have said, "You're going over every minute of your married life together."

He was, of course. ... But Lethbridge did not know why. Lethbridge did not know what Susan had said to him just before she died.

He had stood by the bed looking down at her as she lay unconscious, her face incredibly altered by the last few days' suffering. He was realising that she was dying, and that the children,

3

who had been sent for hurriedly, would probably be too late. And, at the same time, he was trying to believe that it was all a dream from which he was just on the point of awakening. It couldn't be true. . . .

Suddenly she opened her eyes. She was smiling—just as she had smiled at him across the Rectory lawn. A feeling of hysterical relief seized him. It was all right. She couldn't be dying if she smiled at him like that. She began to speak, but so faintly that he had to bend down his head to hear what she said.

"Did you—never guess?"

"What?" he said breathlessly.

"About Charlie—and me."

Then her eyes closed and she lay motionless, as if her looking at him and speaking had been an illusion.

Immediately the door opened, and Lethbridge came in with the nurse and the oxygen tube.

Christopher gave his help mechanically, moving silently and deftly about the sick-room. And, as he moved about the room, the monstrous meaning of the words Susan had said forced itself slowly upon his brain.

They had put aside the oxygen tube now and stood by the bed, looking down at the strange grey face that was Susan's. Lethbridge had his hand on her pulse.

There was silence in the room, but Christopher could still hear the words:

"Did you—never guess—about Charlie and me?"

Suddenly his stunned senses recovered from their paralysis, and a sort of madness seized him. He must know what she meant. Nothing in the whole world mattered but that one thing. He dropped on to his knees by her bed.

"Susan!" he said, "Susan . . . tell me. . . ."

Lethbridge put a hand on his shoulder. "She's gone, old man."

Chapter Two

AT first he had tried to believe that she was delirious, or that, if she were not delirious, in the weakening of her faculties her mind had gone back to some trick that she and Charlie had played on him, and that he had never discovered. Charlie had been fond of practical jokes. Once he had dressed up as an old woman, and had come to consult him in his surgery. Probably he and Susan had played a trick of that sort on him. "Did you never guess about Charlie and me?"

He had even tried to persuade himself that she had never said the words at all, that the whole episode was an illusion of his overwrought nerves. But he could not persuade himself of that, and, as he moved about in a sort of dream, making arrangements for her funeral, interviewing their lawyer, answering letters of condolence, his mind was ceaselessly going over every detail of the days of his friendship with Charles Barrow.

The friendship had been a curious one, for the two men were as unlike in temperament as it is possible almost for two men to be. Christopher was sensitive and reserved, and, in his youth at any rate (they met as medical students at Bart.'s), intensely shy. Charles had been boisterous, full-blooded, instinct with a crude robust joy of life. He lived wholly and vitally in each moment as it passed. He was carelessly kindhearted, prodigally generous, imperturbably good-humoured, and, despite his striking good looks, devoid of vanity.

His friendship with Christopher had been in the nature of an assault. He had simply taken possession of him, ignoring his timidity, laughing at his shyness, overruling his shrinking from intimacy.

After the first surprise Christopher had found it a relief to be thus taken possession of, to have, as it were, a ready-made friendship thrust upon him without the agonies, the heart-searching, the doubts and apprehensions, that in his former experience had been friendship's growing pains. He need not torture himself by fears that Charlie could not possibly like him, because Charlie so obviously did like him; he need not anxiously guard his every shade of manner for fear of hurting Charlie, because Charlie never noticed shades of manner. The friendship had probably been of more value to Christopher than a friendship with a man of his own kind would have been. Charlie's strength had been a corrective to his weakness; Charlie's robust healthy-mindedness a corrective to his tendency to morbidity.

The two had shared rooms, and, when Christopher had obtained his medical degree and removed to his newly-bought practice in Ravenham, he had felt at first curiously lost and bewildered without Charlie. Charlie, too, had qualified, but had not taken up any work. His father had died, leaving him a small estate in Surrey and an ample income, and he had decided to travel abroad for a year or two. It was while he was away that Christopher met and married Susan.

Christopher remembered his feeling of exultant proprietary pride when Charlie appeared a year after their marriage—handsome, exuberant, charming, full of entertaining accounts of his travels, more like a high-spirited school-boy than ever.

The day of that first visit of Charlie's, after his return, stood out vividly in Christopher's memory. Susan had worn a new dress with a tiny waist, a dress that swept in flounces about her feet, and had looked her prettiest. Christopher had watched the two of them with almost breathless eagerness, so great was his anxiety that they should make a good impression on each other. They were the two people he cared for most in the world, and their meeting was of vital importance to him. He could see Charlie quite clearly even now, lounging back in an arm-chair, wholly at his ease, making everything around him look rather small, talking, laughing, his bold twinkling eyes fixed on Susan. He could see Susan, too, seated

gracefully, with her air of poised immobility, on an upright chair, watching Charlie with her faint unfathomable smile. He remembered his relief when Susan told him afterwards that she liked Charlie.
. . .

Charlie had stayed with them for a few days, then, quite suddenly, had gone abroad again and spent two years in Africa. After that he had returned and settled down on his estate in Surrey. He was a frequent week-end visitor to them, and they often spent their holidays with him. Latterly, the old friendship between the two men had waned. Christopher's character had mellowed and strengthened. He had left behind him the introspectiveness and super-sensitiveness of his youth, and, as his need for the virile strength that lay behind them faded, the other man's boisterousness and irresponsibility began to jar on him.

When Charlie had died fifteen years ago, Christopher's sorrow had been more for the friend of his youth than for the man of later years. He had hardly once thought of him since the year of his death, till Susan's words had brought his whole world crashing about him. And then his mind had gone back over those earlier days, groping about among them, dragging back to recollection forgotten words and incidents, trying to light up corners long dim with forgetfulness.

Opportunity? Of course, there had been ample opportunity. The two had been alone in the house evening after evening while he was in his consulting room or out with his cases. They had spent whole days together at Charlie's house in Surrey. And yet, search as it would, his memory could find no evidence against them. They had always welcomed him on his return. They had always seemed glad when he offered to accompany them on their walks or expeditions. When Charlie died, Susan's grief had not been excessive, and all these years she had not mentioned his name.

On the other hand, there had been a vein of dangerous irresponsibility in Charlie. The conventional codes of honour meant little to him. Christopher could imagine his arguing that, as long as he, Christopher, knew nothing of their intrigue, no possible harm was done.

And Susan? He remembered that faint enigmatic smile of hers. Was she, after all, a riddle to which he had failed to find the key, because he had not even realised that there was a key to be found? She had always been withdrawn and aloof, but perhaps she had not really wanted to be withdrawn and aloof. He had treated her throughout their life together with the reverence that had been his first emotion for her, but perhaps she had not wanted to be treated with reverence. Perhaps it was a challenge that he had failed to accept. He had left the glove lying on the ground, and someone else had picked it up. Just as he had found in Charlie what he had missed in himself, so perhaps she had found in Charlie what she had missed in him. . . . Having reached this point, his mind would fly back again into the past, and begin once more to grope in nightmare darkness for something it could not find.

And so the three weeks of his holiday at the Cornish fishing village had slipped by. He went for long walks without seeing anything; he ate his meals from habit and without knowing what he was eating; he lay awake through the long nights, or slipped into heavy unrefreshing sleep made horrible by dreams of Susan and Charlie.

And now he was on his way home. He knew that he was no better. Rather he was worse. He had deliberately let the thing become an obsession.

He must take himself in hand. He was going back to Ravenham now, where people knew him. They must not guess anything. A sudden thought struck him, bringing with it a qualm that was almost physical sickness. Suppose that they knew. Suppose that even his sons and daughter knew.

He put the suspicion behind him, and, with the effort of doing so, a strange new access of strength seemed to come to him. He determined to forget those last few minutes of Susan's life as if they had never been.

Though dreamy, he had his mind and thoughts generally under control. He had always possessed the power of concentration. He would be master of his memories, as a man ought to be. He would think of Susan as he had thought of her till the last few minutes of her life. He would forget Charlie as he had forgotten him these fifteen years. He would believe that Susan had died without recovering consciousness.

A sudden wave of courage and hope swept over him as the train slowed down at Ravenham station.

Chapter Three

THE first thing he saw, when the train drew in, was Lethbridge's long rugged face with its straggling grey goat's beard.

The two men greeted each other casually, almost as if they had met by chance. Both felt constrained and ill-at-ease, though Lethbridge's manner displayed a professional cheerfulness that faintly amused Christopher.

"I just happened to be along," he said, "so I thought I'd pick you up in the car. Got your bag? Splendid."

Lethbridge's car was, in the eyes of some of the inhabitants of Ravenham, a local jest, and, in the eyes of others, a local disgrace. It was of no known make, and had been put together by Lethbridge himself many years before the war. The whole of it, even the nickel of the radiator, was painted a battleship grey. It was very high, and extremely noisy, and, as it had been made long before the days of self-starters, Lethbridge always had to get out to crank it up when it stopped in traffic. He was completely satisfied with it, and nothing would persuade him to exchange it for a more modern make.

Christopher climbed up into it and sank into the deeply hollowed springless seat next to the driver's. The engine started with a roar, Lethbridge took the seat beside him, and they set off noisily through the main street of Ravenham.

Christopher's friendship with Lethbridge was of much later growth than the old friendship with Charlie. It was more a professional than a personal friendship. They discussed their cases unofficially, and, before Christopher's retirement, had frequently called each other in for consultation. Lethbridge was as reserved as Christopher, and they had never been intimate outside their professional spheres;

but, in spite of that, so real was the unspoken understanding between them that it had been to Lethbridge that Christopher's thoughts had first turned in his trouble and bewilderment. Several times, during these weeks since Susan's death, he had played with the idea of confiding in Lethbridge. He thought that if once he could hear Lethbridge's slow steady voice saying, "My dear chap, what *are* you worrying about? It was obviously meaningless delirium. I remember an exactly similar case. . . ."—it would be all right.

But, of course, he could not help knowing that the satisfaction would be short-lived. Lethbridge was a doctor before everything. He told a patient what would help the patient's recovery. Christopher had often heard him say that he considered verbal truthfulness to be a much overrated virtue.

As they drove together through the town from the station in the noisy grey car that seemed to tower so high above the rest of the traffic, Lethbridge's conversation was casual and pleasant, but the glances he threw Christopher were keenly professional.

To Lethbridge, despite their friendship, Christopher was a "case", a man who had been on the edge of a nervous breakdown owing to his wife's death.

"You're looking better, you know," he was saying. "Not yourself, of course. You'll have to be very careful. But you're better."

"Oh, I'm all right," said Christopher lightly, and was conscious of a feeling of relief that he had not confided in Lethbridge. It would have been the end of their friendship. He could never have looked at Lethbridge again without remembering what Susan had said just before she died.

At that thought his mind went back to Charlie, and he had a sudden vivid memory of him leaning over the piano, turning the pages of Susan's music as she played the Chopin waltzes she had always loved. Charlie had a good baritone voice, and was fond of singing comic songs.

Then he thought of his resolution to put the whole thing away from him, and forcibly turned his mind to other matters.

"Tell me," he said to Lethbridge, "how the Cottage Hospital Improvement Fund is getting on."

They discussed the Cottage Hospital Improvement Fund till they reached his house.

Christopher had built the house four years ago, when he retired, giving up his practice to his second son, Frank. He and Susan had talked of his retirement for many years before it actually took place, and had made so many different plans that the thing had become a family joke. Susan's suggestions had ranged from a villa on the Italian Riviera to a cottage on St. Kilda's Island. Christopher, who was conventional, had rather hankered after Bournemouth (he liked the dignified avenued streets and the proximity of the New Forest), but Susan's malicious little jokes made him see it as a sort of rest-home for decayed professional men, so that, even when she relented and said that she would go there if he wanted to, he found that the place had lost its attraction for him.

He was fond of the country and of animals, and for some time they discussed taking a small farm, then Susan had said that he was not retiring in order to go on killing himself with work, and so the idea was dropped. A fair-sized cottage in the country, yet not so deeply buried in the country that Susan could not get up to town for shopping and a *matinée* sometimes, was what they next considered, and they even went to look at one or two in a desultory and half-hearted manner, before they discovered that they did not want to leave their children and the "babies", as Susan called their grandchildren. Having them down for weekends (and the first thing Susan had thought of in all the houses they went over had been where she should put the children and the "babies" when they came to stay) would not be the same thing. They realised, moreover, that they were too old to begin pulling up their roots and making new friends in a new place. The obvious solution was a house just outside Ravenham, as much in the country as possible, but near enough the town for the "babies" to come to tea, as they generally did once a week.

They had spent a dreary month inspecting houses that were too big or too small, houses that had too much garden or too little garden, houses that were too dark, houses without gas or water, well-built houses that were agonizingly hideous, picturesque houses whose roofs let the rain in, houses that were smug and self-satisfied, houses that were sly and evil, houses that were pretentious and suburban, houses without any character at all. And when they had returned, tired and dispirited, from the inspection of a little house with a perfectly useless "musicians' gallery" over a pseudo-Tudor "lounge-hall" panelled in cardboard that took up the entire ground floor, Susan had said suddenly: "We know just what we want. Why not build one ourselves?"

And in less than ten minutes she was talking over the telephone to Merridew, the architect. It was characteristic of Susan that Merridew became as keen on the house as if it had been his own, that he neglected all his other work for it, that he even helped Susan design the garden, drew it out to scale, and stocked it largely with plants from his own borders.

They had decided on a red-brick Georgian house, plain and square, with a roof of Cornish slates, and a green front door beneath a white pediment. There was a long drawing-room with an old-fashioned five-piered bay window, reaching down to the ground and overlooking a terrace and garden at the back of the house. There was a small study for Christopher, and a verandah at the back of the house, so that the "babies" could play there when it was raining.

Susan was like a child with a new toy. She went every day to see how the building was going on. She came to know all the workmen personally, and took a close interest in their families and concerns. Christopher remembered a day when she insisted on going to the house in the pouring rain though she had a bad cold. She said that she wanted to see if they had put the drawing-room mantelpiece in yet, and, when he said that the drawing-room mantelpiece could wait for a fine day, she admitted that her real reason for wanting to go there was that the carpenter's little girl had had her tonsils removed yesterday, and she wanted to know how she was going on, and to give him some grapes for her.

They had been fortunate in the site, a field bordered by a spinney of trees, so that in the summer, when the trees were out, the house could not be seen from the road.

Susan had enjoyed making the garden. When it was finished, she had taken the rock-garden, the rose-garden, and the smaller herbaceous garden under her own charge, and she loved to potter about among them on fine afternoons, wearing an overall and a shady gardening hat, hoeing, weeding, staking, cutting off dead blooms. She said that it was like having another baby.

Christopher's heart began to beat more quickly as the car turned in at the gate between the two oak-trees and entered the dim green drive. The house looked different. It was a house he had never seen before. Nothing about it had been altered since Susan's death—the same curtains hung at the windows, the same furniture could be seen between them—yet it had changed completely. It was a house from which the soul had departed. It was the dead body of a house.

An elderly tight-lipped housemaid, in an unfashionably long skirt and apron, stood at the open door. He was glad that Lydia was there to welcome him. Had the door been shut, he felt that he could never have brought himself to ring the bell or open it with his latch-key. At the cost of concentrating all Lethbridge's professional attention on him, he would have asked him to drive him back to the station.

Lethbridge was murmuring, "Well, good-bye for the present, old chap," and was already beginning to turn his ridiculous grey battleship of a car in the drive.

That proved once more his complete understanding. He knew, as well as Christopher knew, that this home-coming had to be faced alone.

"I thought you'd have come before tea, sir," Lydia was saying, as she closed the door after him.

Her abrupt brusque tone told him more eloquently than any words could have done how real was her sympathy.

Lydia had been with them ever since their marriage. She had been middle-aged and excessively plain when first they had engaged her, and she had remained exactly the same throughout the years, never growing a day older or relaxing an atom of her grimness. Two passions governed her life—economy and classical music. Her passion for economy was an obsession. She would tramp to the other end of the town and back in order to buy groceries for a halfpenny less than she could have bought them nearer home. The fact that her employers could have afforded the extra halfpenny, and would have preferred to pay it, had, in her eyes, no bearing on the case at all. She skimped and cheese-pared because she loved skimping and cheese-paring. There was no trouble she would have shirked in order to make one shilling do the work of two. Her instinct for hoarding was amazing. She could not bear to destroy anything. She kept cupboards full of brown paper and paper bags and string. Susan had once found in a drawer in the kitchen a large box full of used gramophone needles, which evidently she had not been able to bring herself to throw away. She was one of those people to whom the war had been a godsend in the licence that it gave for petty economies. In her housekeeping it had needed all Susan's ingenuity to circumvent her niggardliness. She was as obstinate as she was touchy. At the slightest hint of a reproach she would retire into a gloomy silence that often lasted for several days. She would frequently give a week's notice as an expression of her disapproval of something Susan had said or done, but there the matter was supposed to end. Once Susan, really exasperated with her, had decided that she should go this time, and when the week of her "notice" had expired, ordered a cab for her. Lydia had driven off in it, grim and silent as ever, but with such a look of bewildered panic on her elderly face, that Susan, suddenly relenting, had run down the drive after the cab to bring her back. That was the only time that anyone had seen Lydia cry.

Her love of classical music was the stranger as she was wholly uneducated. She spent all her wages on tickets to symphony concerts, and in her denunciation of "jazz" was like one of the inspired prophets of the Old Testament.

She was so dictatorial with other servants that no one would work with her. Fortunately she enjoyed hard work and preferred to run the house alone with the help of a charwoman. They had long ago given up all thought of getting rid of her.

Christopher entered the hall and looked around him. Susan had kept the house full of flowers—a practice of which Lydia had grimly and silently disapproved. But to-day there were bowls of flowers as usual on the table, desk, and mantelpiece of the hall. They were travesties of Susan's bowls of flowers—stiff, unbending efforts, in which flowers and vases yielded nothing to each other. They were bunches of flowers put into vases and nothing more. It was probably the first time in Lydia's life that she had "arranged" flowers. It touched him to see that she had done it, but the difference between her flowers and Susan's sent again that quick stab of pain through his heart.

"Are you feeling better, sir?" Lydia was saying.

"Much better, thanks, Lydia," he said. "I'm very fit indeed."

His cheerfulness was as much overdone as her brusqueness.

He was stepping towards the drawing-room door, his heart beating thickly. There was something that had to be done, and he must get it over at once. . . . He flung open the door, and faced it—Susan's portrait that formed a panel over the fireplace. It had been painted twenty years ago—in the days when Charlie had almost lived in the house. He remembered that Charlie had suggested a slight alteration in the pose, and that the artist had accepted the suggestion. He closed the door, and stood, his hand still on the handle, looking up at the portrait. The lips were just parted, the eyes alight with a smile that was teasing, enigmatic, tender. It was Susan's very self.

The rest of the room, the pale grey carpet, the gay cretonne covers, the little Queen Anne bureau by the window, the framed embroideries on the walls, seemed only a background for the loveliness and vitality of Susan's portrait. He stood there, silent, motionless, gazing at it, trying to wrest the secret that Susan's eyes withheld. His heart was hammering on his chest, his hand on the doorknob trembled. He was clinging desperately to his determination to forget, and yet suspicions that he would not face seemed to creep about him, so that, even though he shut his eyes to them, he could feel the shadows that they cast. Was it love for Charlie that had thrown that soft bloom upon her? Was the smile in her dark eyes for Charlie? . . . He turned his eyes slowly and reluctantly from the portrait and let them wander round the room, it was a pleasant, companionable room, and he and Susan had used it constantly. But he knew that he would never be able to use it again. He and Susan would not be alone in it any longer. Charlie would always be there now. He went back into the hall, closing the door behind him with fingers that still trembled.

Lydia was waiting with a letter.

"Miss Joy told me to give you this, sir," she said.

He took and opened it.

"DADDY—We thought it best not to bother you just at once when you came home, but our thoughts are with you. We're all coming in after dinner as usual. All our love,

JOY."

The letter sent a warm reassuring glow through his heart.

Chapter Four

"You see," ended Joy, "he thought the brown stuff that the water was filtering through was what softened the water, and it wasn't till he'd been drinking it for a month, and telling everyone that it had practically cured his rheumatism, that he discovered that the brown stuff was sawdust, and only meant for packing, and should have been taken out before the thing was put up, and that the water wasn't softened at all, because he'd never put any salt in it. . . ."

Derek laughed uproariously from his corner by the book-case. Frank joined in the laughter less enthusiastically. Olivia and Rachel smiled—bright conspiratorial smiles that loyally supported Joy in her efforts to make this first meeting without Susan seem less strange and gloomy.

Bruce, Joy's husband, was not there. One of his aunts had sent for him, because her accounts had "got into a muddle", and he had gone to straighten them out.

Bruce had innumerable aunts, and was a very dutiful nephew. He filled in their Income-Tax Forms for them, audited their accounts, and looked out trains for them when they were going on journeys. As a natural result, they blamed him when anything went wrong, but took the credit to themselves when their affairs went smoothly.

Christopher had told Lydia to put the coffee and sandwiches in his study instead of the drawing-room. The study held the furniture that had been in his old surgery: two big cupboards with book-cases on the top, a writing-desk, leather arm-chairs, a shabby leather couch, and framed photographs of school and college groups on the walls.

The moment of pouring out the coffee had been a difficult one. Susan had had a way of presiding over a tea-table that made "pouring out" a sort of ceremonial. She had leant slightly forward in her chair, arranging the cups and saucers on the tray slowly, gracefully, abstractedly, as if every movement were important, and at once the whole room seemed to be drawn into a magic circle of warmth and comfort.

Christopher realised that Joy had been tactful. She had made no attempt to imitate Susan, nor had she hurried over the proceeding, as if it were something painful to be got over as quickly as possible. She had done it in her own way—a brisk, business-like, mother-of-a-young-family way, that somehow reassured them and set them at their ease.

They had finished now, and Lydia had come in to clear away. She was doing it in her most aggressive manner, clattering the china together angrily, banging the door when she went out. They knew that her anger-was directed not against them, but against the fate that had taken Susan from them. They heard her moving about, still angrily and noisily, in the kitchen; then they heard faint strains of Schubert's Unfinished Symphony, and could imagine her leaning back in her shabby basket-chair—she had always refused to have it replaced by a new one—near the kitchen wireless, her eyes shut, her mouth open. Frank, as a boy, had been able to give side-splitting imitations of Lydia's face when listening to classical music.

A sudden silence fell, and Christopher, feeling that he was not doing his share in relieving the strain, turned to Frank and said:

"Things going all right?"

Frank evidently felt that it was not the right moment for a serious discussion of the practice. He began to tell them about Mrs. West, who, thinking that her little boy looked pale at tea-time, had thrust a thermometer into his mouth and found that it registered 104°. She put him to bed at once, and telephoned distractedly for Frank.

"I went round, took the kid's temperature, and found it normal. She simply wouldn't believe me. She kept showing me her thermometer, and saying that mine must be out of order. So I took it with hers, and still it was normal. You see, she'd plunged it into the kid's mouth without waiting for him to swallow his bread and milk. . . . She'd wired for her husband to come home from Scotland before I got there, and she'd rung up all her relations to say that he was seriously ill. I met an aunt coming in as I went away, with a basket of grapes on one arm, and a bed-table on the other. . . ."

They all laughed again—Derek uproariously. Derek loved stories that savoured slightly of the practical joke.

And, suddenly, everything seemed quite normal and natural. The strangeness had gone from the situation. The usual desultory family conversations arose—conversation about children, neighbours, pieces of local news. Christopher could relax his efforts, and watch them detachedly.

He had been on excellent terms with his children while they were in the nursery, but, as they grew up, he had begun to feel the same shyness and reserve with them that he felt with other people. He felt, indeed, an added diffidence with them, as if half-ashamed of the conventional authority that the relationship gave him, and anxious not to presume on it. As they emerged from childhood, they had seemed to grow away from him. They had never been necessary to him as they had been necessary to Susan.

Derek had been Susan's favourite. He was the best-looking of the three, with crisp fair hair, grey-blue eyes, straight nose, and a well-formed cleft chin. His pouting lips, the lower one slightly protruding, alone marred his beauty. Sometimes Christopher had wondered whether it were subconscious jealousy—for he was not conscious of feeling jealous—that had made him care less for Derek than for the other two. Of late years, in fact, Derek had jarred on him so much that he had consciously avoided him. He was talking to Frank now, raising his voice:

"I heard of the stuff going cheap and bought it up. I ought to clear two or three hundred on it. . . . Barlow's have given me a bigger order than they have ever given me before. Barlow came to dinner with us last month, you know. His father's Sir James Barlow, the baronet. I was telling him that Olivia and I were thinking of moving into the country. I was looking at Helston Court last week. . . ."

Christopher, listening, was conscious of a familiar irritation. They all knew that Derek could not afford to take Helston Court. He had told them about Barlow's coming to dinner with him a dozen times already. If he said he would clear two or three hundred, it probably meant fifty pounds at most. He was hardly responsible for what he said when he began to talk like this. Christopher had a curious feeling that most of it was aimed at him, as if Derek were dimly conscious of his disapproval and determined to overcome it. Derek could not endure criticism and, like all self-centred people, lacked perception. It was his lack of perception that made him so frequently try to impress his own family as if they were strangers, try to force them to see him as he saw himself. He never knew when his audience was out of sympathy with him. He obviously did not sense the atmosphere now: Frank and Joy amused, Christopher faintly hostile, Olivia—one never knew what Olivia felt. Only Rachel, Frank's wife, was slightly, very slightly, impressed.

Susan would not have been irritated by him. She would have seen a little boy planting sturdy bare legs far apart and saying: "I met a hundred lions in the garden and I killed them all dead."

And, of course, he would not have been quite like this if Susan had been there. Susan could always check him by a smile, a word, when he began to be outrageous.

Christopher glanced again at Olivia, who sat silent and motionless by the window, her dark graceful head turned towards Derek. He remembered his secret relief when Derek told him that he was engaged to Olivia. Derek was so susceptible to flattery that they had been afraid of his making a foolish marriage. When he married Olivia, they had felt that all danger was over, that everything would go well.

Now, seeing the look in her dark eyes as she watched Derek, Christopher suddenly wasn't sure.

Frank was listening to Derek with a twinkle that made him seem almost a school-boy again. Frank and Derek had never got on well, though Frank's good-temper made him impossible to quarrel with. Physically, Derek could have asked no better foil than Frank. He was a head shorter than Derek, thick-set and ungraceful. His face was swarthy, his hair coal-black, wiry, and unmanageable, but there was a disarming friendliness in his eyes, and the corners of his big mouth were full of generosity and humour.

Though a merry affectionate boy, he had somehow always been the "odd man out" in the family. He had been so popular at school and college that, once his school-days had begun, they had seen little of him at home. He had not seemed to need either of them, as Joy had consciously needed Christopher, and Derek had unconsciously needed Susan. For Derek's conceit and self-importance were always being wounded, and, without knowing it, he had continual need of Susan's tenderness.

Frank, on the other hand, had been so independent in spirit and so sound in body that they had never felt for him that protective anxiety that is the deepest bond between parent and child. His popularity made his school and college days a sort of triumphal progress. He had left college with an excellent medical degree, and had entered his career as a doctor with hope and confidence. Then, suddenly and inexplicably, the triumphal progress had come to an end. He was well-meaning and hard-working, but he lacked the indefinable something that makes a doctor successful. He was casual, almost off-hand, in manner, and, despite his innate kindliness, devoid of tact. The qualities that had made him popular with his fellow-students failed to make him popular with his patients. He was aware of his lack of success, and it troubled and perplexed him. He had had Christopher's old practice only a few years now, and it was already dwindling slowly, but unmistakably.

It was not only Frank, of course, thought Christopher. Ravenham had grown, and professional competition had increased. There had been three doctors there when Christopher bought his practice, and now there were twelve, beside the two women doctors, who had come to the town and were working up large practices. Moreover, the heyday of the family doctor was over. Money was scarce, and people no longer consulted doctors about trifles. They bought patent medicines and doctored themselves. They changed their doctors, too, for any reason or no reason. In Christopher's young days, people did not change their doctors. A name on a doctor's books meant a patient for life. ... Christopher's gaze wandered from Frank to Rachel. Rachel, of course, was not much help to a man. ...

Joy was talking about her children. "It was the first time she'd seen an unsharpened pencil, and she said: 'Oh, look, Mummy, a pencil without a beak,' " and Frank was looking at Rachel with a familiar expression of anxiety.

Rachel's dark eyes were smouldering, her red lips set. It was torment to Rachel to be left out of a conversation. It infuriated her to hear Joy talking about her children ("as if they were the only children in the world!"). She would not make any effort to enter the conversation, she would not even allow herself to be drawn into it. Once that feeling of being ignored and despised came upon her, she shut herself up into a little hell of her own making and refused to come out.

"His hands were filthy before we'd been in the railway carriage for five minutes," Joy was saying, in her laughing voice, "and I said he wasn't to *touch* his face with them. Then I saw him making the most frightful faces, and I said 'What *is* the matter, Billy?' and he said: 'I'm trying to scratch my nose with my teeth.' "

"Do tell Father what Barbara said the other day, Rachel," said Frank.

But it was too late, and too obvious.

"I've forgotten," said Rachel shortly. "I've other things to think of than what the children say and do."

"Oh do, Rachel," said Joy, trying to help Frank.

"I've forgotten," said Rachel again, and set her red lips more tightly.

Then Derek began to talk about his new car. It was, according to Derek, a far better car in every way than any other car on the market, even one that cost three times as much. The glamour that covered Derek in his own eyes, extended to all his possessions.

Joy shot a quick fugitive smile at Christopher, a smile that laughed at the childishness of Rachel and Derek, that pitied Frank, and sent a message of sympathy and consolation to Christopher himself.

Yet, even as she smiled, there was a preoccupied look on her face, as if her real thoughts were elsewhere. She had worn that preoccupied look ever since she married Bruce.

Joy had always been Christopher's favourite. When she was a little girl he had literally adored her, and throughout her childhood they had been close friends. In spite of his busy life, he had always found time to share her games and interests. He never had to "play down" to her, because he was at heart essentially a child. The games and imaginings of childhood were real to him. He enjoyed the books of the nursery—*Brer Rabbit, Alice in Wonderland, The Just So Stories*—far more than what Joy called "grown-up" books.

Joy had loved him almost as passionately as he loved her. He had formed her whole world in those days. Looking at her now, he seemed to see her as a little girl entering the doorway of the drawing-room, where he and Susan had just finished tea, the battered toy-monkey that was her invariable companion tucked under her arm, her golden hair brushed to the side like a boy's, her rosy, shining, little, face wreathed in smiles of anticipatory delight at the thought of the hour of games and romps before bed-time.

There had been something eager and sweet and trusting and defenceless about her, that even now, in memory, tugged at his heart. Looking back, those days of Joy's little girlhood seemed to him the happiest days of his life.

They had soon passed, of course. She had left the world of childhood and entered another world where he could not follow her—a world of dances and boy friends, of parties, of modern plays and books and music. She still loved him, but a slight suggestion of amused tolerance had entered into her affection for him. ("Daddy's such an old-fashioned darling, you know.") It was Susan who was nearest to her now. Then came her marriage with Bruce Ranger—a marriage that had been a bitter disappointment to Christopher. Bruce, insignificant both in appearance and intellect, had seemed the last man in the world who should have been Joy's husband. He was not even well off. They could not possibly have managed without the two hundred a year that had been left to Joy by Susan's sister. The amazing thing was that, though they had been married for nine years, they were still in love with each other.

Always when Joy was away from her home she wore that pre-occupied look as if she were not really there. She wasn't there, of course. . . . She was at home, giving the children their tea, bathing the baby, putting Bruce's slippers ready for him by the fire. Christopher could not pretend now that he was anything to Joy except a "dear old thing", who was going to be rather a responsibility, now that Susan was dead.

They had returned to the safe subject of local news, and were telling him about old Bellamy's bankruptcy. Rachel, of course, was taking no part in the discussion. She was still shut away in her little private hell, fulfilling the dual role of torturer and tortured. ("They don't want me. . . . They all hate me. . . . No one in the world wants me. . . . I wish I'd never been born.") Frank was taking part in the discussion half-heartedly, anxiously, waiting and watching for an opportunity to bring Rachel into it in such a way that she would forget her little hell, but knowing that it was hopeless, that whatever he did or said would only make things worse.

"I'm very sorry for them," he was saying. "It seems a shame that it should have happened to them. Mrs. Bellamy's helped in almost every social work in Ravenham, hasn't she, Rachel?"

He caught a look of agonised reproach from Rachel, and remembered, too late, that to praise another woman was, in Rachel's eyes, to blame her.

"She can't have had much to do at home," she said in an unsteady voice, "or she wouldn't have had time for social work."

"Bruce says . . ." began Joy, with that faint preoccupied smile on her lips.

Then the clock struck ten, and there was a sudden atmosphere of relaxing. The evening was over. Next time things would be less difficult. The new tone of the meeting had been set, the new relations established. And with the sudden easing of the strain, the guard that Christopher had set upon his memory broke down. "Did you never guess about Charlie and me?" Forget? He had been mad to think that he could forget. A hot feeling of suffocation came over him, and his heart began to beat unevenly. He must know; he must find out somehow. He could not go on like this, wondering, suspecting, wavering to and fro.

He remembered suddenly the box of letters and papers of Susan's that he had shut away in the cupboard in their bedroom after her death. He had not been able to bring himself to go through them. He would go through them to-night. . . . He could hardly restrain his impatience, while the children collected their wraps, took affectionate farewells of him, and set off—Frank in his battered old Morris Oxford, and Derek in the smart new two-seater.

He called out "Good-night" to Lydia, and went upstairs, his heart still beating rapidly. In the bedroom he turned the key in the lock, then slowly and deliberately opened the cupboard door, and took out the box of letters.

Chapter Five

OLIVIA raised her eyes and gave her husband a keen appraising glance, as he entered the dining-room, and, without looking at her, took his place at the other end of the breakfast table. His pouting lips were set in a sullen line, and there was a deep furrow between his brows.

She filled his coffee cup and passed it to him across the table. He took it from her, still in silence, and, after glancing through his letters, began to eat his breakfast, his eyes fixed on his plate.

In the silence, her thoughts went back to the days when these moods of his had filled her with sick misery, when she had sat digging her nails into the palms of her hands, praying for them to pass, and the radiance of his love and pleasure in her to return.

Well, those days were over. Her love for him had died a slow and painful death. His ill-humour could weary and depress her, but it could not hurt her any more. Almost she would rather have him like this, than in those moods when, feeling pleased with himself and the world and wanting the old flattering confidence of her adoration, he tried to make love to her.

He jerked his head suddenly from his paper, and fixed his scowling gaze on her.

"You're a pleasant companion, aren't you?" he said.

It was clear that he could not keep his savageness to himself any longer. She braced herself for the inevitable scene.

"I spoke to you several times upstairs," she said quietly, "and you wouldn't answer me."

He took an envelope from the pile by his plate and tossed it over to her.

"You won't be satisfied, I suppose, till you've completely ruined me."

She opened it. It was the bill—still unpaid—for his new two-seater, with a note respectfully requesting an early settlement of the account. She put it back in the envelope and returned it to him without comment.

"It's been one thing after another," he shot out viciously. "You must have this, you must have that. . . . You drove me into buying this car, because you thought the old one wasn't good enough for you. You gave me no peace till I'd bought it. Now, perhaps, you'll be good enough to tell me where the money's coming from."

She was accustomed to his putting the blame on her whenever he bought something that he could not afford. She answered with a faint impatience but without surprise or rancour.

"I never asked you to buy the car, Derek. If you remember, I even advised you not to."

He ignored the remark and continued stormily—"If I do go smash, you'll be entirely responsible. No man can possibly do justice to his business when he's being drained by an extravagant wife. I've given you everything you wanted, and, now that your extravagance has ruined me, I hope you're satisfied."

The almost incredible part of it was that he honestly believed what he said. He never lied deliberately. He possessed an amazing faculty for inventing what he wanted to remember, and then actually remembering it.

Nor did he really dislike her. He was, in his own way, fond of her, and considered himself an excellent husband. Only when things went wrong, she was the obvious and legitimate outlet for his annoyance.

She looked at him in silence, wondering exactly how his affairs stood. He would never confide in her, because he hated to admit failure of any sort. One of his delusions was that he was a business genius.

"Derek, please be frank with me," she said suddenly. "If you want me to economise, of course, I will. We can easily do without

Florrie. I could help with the work. Cook and I together could manage perfectly. If the business isn't doing well—"

He interrupted, flaming out at her in sudden anger.

"You'll kindly mind your own business, and I'll mind mine. I'm perfectly capable of looking after my business. The business is all right. It's your extravagance that's wrong."

"I'm not extravagant, Derek, and I've offered to economise even more than I do. I can give Florrie notice to-day."

Her answer irritated him, and he began to lose control of himself.

"That's like you," he shouted. "There's nothing you'd like better than to humiliate me publicly. You want to set the whole town gossiping about my affairs—saying that we can't afford to keep a housemaid."

She shrugged wearily, rose from her seat, and went out into the hall. She was used to his anger, and she was not frightened of him, yet it always set her heart beating unevenly.

She entered the morning-room where Florrie was sweeping the carpet with the vacuum cleaner, and began to give her directions about the morning's work.

Derek, who had followed her, strode suddenly into the room, his handsome face still black, and turned off the electric switch.

"Haven't you any more sense," he stormed, "than to leave that on while you stand and gossip? I suppose it's news to you that electricity costs money?"

She flushed hotly. He had never before spoken to her like that in front of the servants. He went out again, and the sound of the front door banging behind him re-echoed through the house.

She finished her conversation with Florrie as if nothing had happened, then went upstairs to her bedroom. There she closed the door, and stood still for a moment, consciously enjoying its peace and silence. He would be away till this evening now. That was one comfort. There were two photographs of Derek on the mantelpiece. One of them had been taken just before their marriage. His face still wore the mask of youth. There were no revealing lines of character upon it. It might have been the "heroic head" of a Hellenistic sculpture. Even the slight pout of the full lips was rather attractive than otherwise. She could never look at it without remembering the brief madness of her passion for him. The other photograph had been taken a year ago. The mask of youth had withdrawn itself. The eyes had lost their look of eager ingenuousness. The pouting lips held ill-humour and a hint of complacency.

Olivia's gaze went from one to the other, and her mouth twisted into a bitter smile.

The trouble with Derek was that he considered himself to be so much more brilliant in every way than he really was. His good-looks were, of course, exceptional, but he took for granted that he possessed every other desirable quality, mental and moral, to a commensurate degree, and he was perpetually being hurt and affronted by proofs that other people did not see him as he saw himself. He had set up a sort of image of himself that he worshipped, and that he expected everyone else to worship, too.

Olivia knew that it was her failure to worship the Image any more, that was at the root of their growing alienation. Once, of course, the Image had had no more devout worshipper than she. . . .

Her mind went back to this morning's scene. He had very little self-control, and would often vent a passing mood of depression on her in a burst of irritability, but his anger this morning, she realised uneasily, went deeper than that. She had suspected for some weeks that things were going badly with his business.

There was something faintly ludicrous about the whole history of his business career. When he left college, he had chosen to read for the Bar, but he had tired of it in a year, and, on the advice of a casual acquaintance, had bought a small paper-manufacturing business. It was characteristic of Derek to take the advice of a casual acquaintance, rather than that of anyone more intimately connected with him. It was quite a good business, though perhaps not worth what he gave for it. He had been full of confidence. The Image, of course, was to have no ordinary business career. It was to be a "paper king", a millionaire, a figure of international importance.

As Derek possessed no business experience whatever, it was

fortunate for him that he had agreed to retain the manager of the business—an ugly little man, called Sefton, who spoke with a Cockney accent and dropped his h's, but who proved himself more than a match for his employer. Cunningly he circumvented Derek's preposterous plans, purposely misunderstood his orders, and kept the business running on sound old-fashioned lines, expanding very gradually and very safely, consolidating its position at each step, where Derek would have ruined it in a week. Derek had chafed under his control. He saw himself standing with one foot poised on the ladder, ready to step into the position he had outlined for himself. He had it all planned—the country house, the town house, the villa on the Riviera, the yacht, photographs and interviews in the newspapers. He loved to refer to his go-ahead revolutionary business methods, but some subconscious instinct of safety had made him keep Sefton with him till six months ago. Then his patience had finally given out, and, discovering that Sefton had deliberately disobeyed an order that would have wasted half the available capital of the firm, he had given him notice. Sefton had accepted it without comment or protest, and had quietly left the firm. Derek had been exultant and triumphant.

"I was a fool not to do it years ago," he had said to Olivia. "He's kept the business back all this time. Now I can get ahead!"

"Derek, you'll be careful, won't you?" she had said apprehensively.

"Oh, my dear girl," he had replied, with a tolerant smile, "don't try to teach me how to run a business."

He had been jubilant and confident for several weeks, and then his mood of ill-humour had descended on him, becoming blacker and blacker, till—as this morning—she seemed to catch sight of a panic fear behind it.

She had known that things were bad last night. She had not been deceived by his cheerfulness and boasting at his father's. The presence of other people, even his own family, always acted as a sort of stimulant on Derek, making him forget his worries, and see only the Image—handsome, charming, successful.

Her thoughts went back again to this morning's scene. He had never before been quite so outrageous as that. Perhaps his mother's death had something to do with it. He had not consciously grieved for her, but there was a spoilt little boy in Derek that only his mother could manage. He had always been at his best with her. Perhaps her death had removed some check of which he had been only half conscious. . . .

She roused herself from her reverie, put on her hat and coat, and set off to do her morning's shopping.

Chapter Six

As she walked down High Street, she still felt depressed. It was not only Derek's ill-humour. It was the memory of Derek's father last night, that kept returning to her. She really loved the old man, and he had looked so worn, so tired, so old, so indescribably pathetic. It was pitiful to think of him left alone like this.

Some men could love their wives, and yet, somehow, seem independent of them. Derek's father had not been like that. He had depended utterly on Susan. For years they had seldom been seen apart. Susan's charm had been delicate, elusive, all pervading. It was impossible not to love her.

A vivid memory of Susan's face came to her—the silvery hair, the blue eyes, the cheeks as soft as a young girl's, the lips with their faint mysterious smile. Always that something withdrawn about her, that hint of mockery beneath her tenderness, that faint acerbity behind her sweetness, that barbed keenness in her wit. It must be terrible for a man who had lived with Derek's mother to have to learn to live without her. Her mind went back in imagination over their past. She thought of that glowing portrait of Susan as a young woman that hung over the mantelpiece in the drawing-room of Christopher's house. . . . They must have been very very happy together.

A sudden pang of envy shot through her heart. She took her shopping list from her bag, and stared at it dreamily, without seeing anything.

Fifty years ago, Ravenham had been a small country town, but it had expanded until, rather to its surprise, it found itself joined to the line of suburbs that had crept out from London. It was still surrounded by country on the other three sides, but the road to London was now a continuous stretch of shops and houses. The last fields on the London side of Ravenham had disappeared two years ago, and were still in the course of being "developed" as a housing estate. Last year, too, the railway had been electrified, and a twenty-minute service to the City and Victoria instituted. New and palatial branches of big combines were replacing the modest premises of the old family tradesmen, who used themselves to serve behind their counters, and know all their customers personally. The market-place to which, fifty years ago, farmers from the outlying country places brought their products, and where rosy-cheeked farmer's wives sat behind stalls of butter and eggs and cheese and bacon, was full now of cheap-jacks from the east end of London: hawkers, shoddy auctioneers, fortune tellers, and purveyors of balloons, silk stockings, highly coloured sweets, glittering "jewelry", flashy clothing of all kinds.

Yet something of the old character of the town remained. Dignified Georgian houses (mostly occupied now by professional men) still stood sedately here and there among the shops of High Street. And, even among the shops, the small old-fashioned establishments where Mr. Walker still supervised in person the making of his cakes (Mr. Walker said that the blackest day of life had been the day when he had had to substitute margarine for butter during the war), where Mrs. Bolton still made her famous treacle toffee and mint humbugs, where Mr. Granger in white apron served the best English groceries, where Mr. Pollock, the butcher, resplendent in striped apron, could tell you which local farm had supplied each joint, held their own easily among the upstart palaces. The palaces had their clientele, of course, but the best people remained faithful to Mr. Walker, Mrs. Bolton, Mr. Granger, Mr. Pollock.

It was the woman's hour in Ravenham. Smart young housewives were hurrying in and out of the shops, forming groups on the pavements, or sitting round the tables of the little cafés drinking coffee to a pleasant accompaniment of cigarettes and gossip. Prams and dogs on leads formed a large part of every group. Rows of motor-cars stood in the unofficial parking-place by the parish church, the July sunshine glittering on polished radiators and well-groomed wings, and among them strutted the presiding genius of the place—a tiny man, dressed in clothes many sizes too big for him, who made strange movements with his arms, windmill-like and unintelligible, whenever a car approached. Along the kerb the baskets of flower hawkers made bright patches of colour in High Street.

The dual character of the little town could be seen in the clothes of the women. Country tweeds and brogues were as much in evidence as toilets suggestive of Bond Street.

Olivia was just passing the Baptist chapel, on whose steps an old man sat all day making 3d. kettle-holders, when she met Joy wheeling a perambulator in which Bobs lay asleep.

Joy looked as ever faintly pre-occupied.

"One always meets everyone in High Street this time of the morning, doesn't one," said Joy absently. "How are you?"

"Splendid, thanks."

"And Derek?"

"Splendid," said Olivia.

"Last night went off awfully well, I thought, didn't you?"

"At your father's. . . . Yes, I suppose it did."

"I think he's got over it wonderfully."

"He doesn't look well."

"Oh, I think he does," said Joy. "It was a dreadful shock, of course. But I thought he seemed wonderfully cheerful and happy."

Joy had no time for other people's troubles, thought Olivia, and so she persuaded herself that they hadn't any. . . . Happy people were always selfish.

"I've been to Barrat's," went on Joy, "to get Bobs some new shoes. She wanted the red ones, but they weren't quite big enough so she had to have the brown. It's such comfort being able to fit the children's shoes by X-rays. It used to be so hopeless. . . . They'd tell you they were comfortable in the shop, and the very next day they'd say they were hurting. Dickie used to be *awful*. Well, I must get Bobs home. She can't sleep properly in the town. The motor-horns are always waking her up."

"I suppose so," said Olivia, without looking at Bobs. "Good-bye."

She went on alone through the crowd. Sometimes the sight of Joy's babies did not give her this strange pain at her heart, but sometimes it did. When it did, she had to try not to look at them or think of them. It was so foolish to let one's thought dwell on a thing that could not be helped. No one, of course, had ever known how passionately she had longed for a child. Derek had not really wanted one. He had been vaguely sorry for her when the first child had been born dead, but that was all. When the second child had been born dead, and the doctor had told her that she would never be able to bear a living child, he had been slightly relieved, because he had found her pregnancy inconvenient. She had tried to put the thought of children definitely away from her then, to make herself forget that she had ever wanted them, but it had not been easy, and even now, after all these years, the sight of Bobs asleep in her pram like this could send a sharp stab of pain through her heart.

She saw little Mrs. Maydew, but too late to avoid her.

"*Darling!*" cried little Mrs. Maydew, swooping down upon her. "How *lovely* to see you. It's *ages* since I saw you, and I've been thinking of you *such* a lot. *How* are you and *how's* everything? I'm simply *longing* to hear your news, darling. Come and have coffee with me, and tell me everything about everything. I've got simply *heaps* to tell you."

Little Mrs. Maydew greeted all her acquaintances, even the most casual ones, in this way. She came into town every morning, accosting with enthusiasm such of her acquaintances as did not see her in time to avoid her, till she had found someone to have coffee with her, then she would sit in her own particular alcove in her own particular café being cloyingly affectionate and embarrassingly confidential, till it was time to go home to lunch.

Olivia excused herself, and hurried on. Behind her she heard a scream of "*Darling!*" as little Mrs. Maydew accosted another acquaintance.

She thought she caught sight of Rachel in Boots, but she was not sure, and did not try to find her. One never quite knew how

Rachel would receive one. Sometimes she was pleasant, even affectionate, and at other times she would hardly speak. It was safer to avoid her as far as possible. In-law relatives are difficult, thought Olivia, as she paid her bill and went out of Boots. It was so ridiculous to be expected to be on terms of intimate friendship with some one with whom you had not a single taste or interest in common, just because you happened to have married their husband's brother. . . .

She felt tired when she reached home, but her walk into the town and back had cheered her. Her lunch of cold meat and salad stood waiting on the table. She had ordered a roast chicken for dinner, to be followed by pine-apple cream sponge and a savoury. When Derek was in this mood, a lot depended on the dinner. A good dinner would often save the household from an unpleasant evening.

The telephone bell rang while she was giving the cook final instructions, and she went into the morning-room to answer it.

"Yes?"

"Olivia?"

Her heart began to beat quickly.

"Yes . . . it's Stephen, isn't it?"

"Yes. I want to come to see you. May I come to tea?"

"Yes. Come at four. Don't be late."

"Rather not. Good-bye."

"Good-bye."

She hung back the receiver. All her depression had vanished. A calm radiance of happiness possessed her.

Chapter Seven

RACHEL walked slowly down the High Street, her brows drawn together tensely. Olivia had cut her. She had seen her in Boots, then turned hastily away, pretending not to see her. Rachel's heart was a seething tumult of anger and misery. She did not care for Olivia (she rather disliked her, in fact), but she felt as wretched as if her dearest friend had betrayed her, as angry as if Olivia had deliberately and publicly insulted her. All Rachel's emotions were like that—intense, exaggerated, unutterably wearing to herself and those around her.

The day had begun badly. Or rather the origin of the trouble had been last night. Her thoughts turned back now angrily, broodingly, to last night. Frank's people had never liked her, of course, but they had never shown their dislike quite as openly as they had shown it last night. Hardly one of them had spoken to her. Frank had tried to defend them when they got home. He had said that it was a difficult occasion—their first meeting without his mother. She had told him that that was no excuse for purposely leaving her out of the conversation. It had never been like that when Frank's mother was alive. Frank's mother had liked her. She always came to sit by her and talk to her. She always took an interest in what she had been doing, complimented her on anything new she was wearing, remembered to ask if the new curtains were a success, or if the washing-machine was working better, or how her mother and sister were—little things, but things she would never have thought of asking if she had not liked her and taken an interest in her. She had done her hair a different way last night, and neither Olivia nor Joy had mentioned it. They must have noticed it. Their not saying anything about it was, of course, a deliberate unkindness. To her distorted imagination, the whole party seemed a preconcerted plot to make her feel out of it, to prove to her how much they all disliked her. To make things worse, this morning, while they dressed, Frank had defended them, finding excuses for them, ranging himself with them against her. . . .

Mrs. Haines, who was just going into Granger's, her eyes fixed on a shopping list, looked up as Rachel passed and nodded absently with a preoccupied smile. The wave of angry misery flooded Rachel's heart again. Even Mrs. Haines disliked her and didn't care how plainly she showed it.

She went into Pollock's, her lips compressed, her cheeks flushed, her dark eyes smouldering. The assistant was deferential and humble, keeping a wary eye upon her. Mrs. Frank Mainwaring was known to change her tradesmen pretty frequently. She was known also to complain to managers of insolence from assistants on very little provocation. He accepted her complaint that the last joint had been tough with expressions of shocked surprise and deep contrition. His concern and his frequent repetition of "Madam", were vaguely soothing, and she went into the street feeling calmer. But at the door she met Mrs. Haines again, and that reminded her of the slight that she had just received from her. Mrs. Haines, who had solved the problem of the entry on her shopping list that had been puzzling her, looked at Rachel with a bright smile, but Rachel passed her quickly with head averted. People couldn't play fast and loose with her like that, she told herself fiercely, cutting her one minute and smiling at her the next. . . . If Mrs. Haines didn't want to know her, she needn't. . . . As she walked home her anger left her, but her depression increased till it was like a thick black cloud choking her, like a heavy weight to which she was chained, and which she could hardly drag along with her. Her mind returned to her original grievance, and she felt an angry revulsion from Frank and his family. They were aliens, they had no part in her. Her memory went back to her childhood. She saw herself and Violet sitting at their mother's feet on the hearthrug, while her mother read aloud to them. She watched the firelight flickering on to Violet's delicately lovely little face. These were her people, not Frank and his family. But the picture was vaguely unsatisfying. Her mother lived in Bournemouth now, and Violet was married to a man who disliked Rachel almost as much as Rachel disliked him. Then her thoughts turned to Jonathan and Barbara, her children, with a hungry intensity. They were hers, they belonged to her. They were the only beings in the world who loved her. Their love must make up for everything. . . .

She was standing at the front door smiling when they returned from school. Jonathan was a slim, tall boy of nine, with a sharp, thin Puck's face, and quick jerky movements. Barbara was a fat solemn little girl of seven, with a round face, brown eyes, dark curls, and a warm sleepy voice. Jonathan slowed his pace as he approached the front door. He was acutely sensitive to his mother's moods, and had noticed something strained in her smile as soon as he saw her. He entered the house watching her warily. She dropped on to her knees as he entered and clasped him tightly to her. He could feel the tenseness of her emotion, as if it were something nauseating, suffocating. He stiffened and tried to push her away from him.

"Jonathan!" she cried. "What's the matter, darling? Why are you like that with Mummy? You love her, don't you?"

It was like something trying to get hold of every bit of him, to leave nothing of him at all for himself.

He stood taut and unresponsive in her embrace, still straining away from her. Her smile grew fixed and unnatural. She was trying to control herself, not to let him see that she was upset, but his repulse of her was torture.

"Tell Mummy you love her," she persisted.

She tried to speak lightly, laughingly, but Jonathan's small tense figure did not relax. He felt as if he were fighting against being drowned in the turbid waves of her emotion.

"You're hurting me, Mummy."

She relaxed her hold.

"I'm sorry, darling. I'm not hurting you now, am I? Just tell Mummy that you love her."

It was better now that he wasn't pressed close to her. The frightening choking feeling had gone. But he pursed his lips obstinately. She wanted him to belong to her altogether, and, though he loved her, he didn't want to belong to her altogether. He wanted to belong to himself. She wanted to know everything he thought and felt. She wanted him to be thinking of her all the time, to be loving her all the time. And he wouldn't ... he couldn't. So he stood reluctant in her embrace, looking away from her without speaking. He knew that she would leave him alone if he did that. Her eyes were bright with misery, her breast rising and falling unevenly, as she turned to Barbara.

"*You* love Mummy, don't you, sweetheart?"

The little roly-poly that was Barbara put her arms round Rachel's neck and said in her sweet, sleepy voice, "Yes, Mummy."

Barbara was matter-of-fact and imperceptive. She was not sensitive to Rachel's moods as Jonathan was. Rachel was just Mummy to her, sometimes cross, and sometimes not cross, as all Mummies were. Barbara never connected the crossness or not-crossness with anything but her and Jonathan's behaviour. If they were "naughty", Mummy was cross; if they were "good", Mummy was pleased with them. Jonathan had long ago noticed that when Mummy was in one mood everything they did was "naughty", and when she was in another they were "good" and "darlings" whatever they did. His attitude to her was one of caution. He gave her as little as he could because she was greedy, and he knew that if he gave her anything she would try to take more. He had a queer half-unconscious understanding of her.

"Go and wash your hands for lunch, darling," said Rachel tenderly to Barbara, who was still clinging to her, and added coldly to Jonathan, "Go and wash your hands."

She ignored Jonathan when they came in to lunch, and gave her whole attention to Barbara, talking to her, and making her a little pond of gravy in her mashed potatoes. She behaved, in fact, as if Jonathan were not there at all, passing him his plate without looking at him or speaking to him. Her smile, as she talked to Barbara, was strained and fixed. There was, after all, very little satisfaction in Barbara's response. Barbara was so docile, so universally affectionate. Her petting of Barbara was not for Barbara's sake, it was for Jonathan's, to punish him for having repulsed her. As Jonathan watched them, a hot flame of jealousy sprang up in his heart. He hated her kissing him and fussing over him, but he could not bear to see her doing it to Barbara and ignoring him. He began deliberately to misbehave, eating noisily and kicking the table leg.

Rachel turned to him. "Don't do that, Jonathan."

He stopped kicking the table leg, and began to sing as he ate. Rachel turned from Barbara again with a sharp. "Jonathan, behave yourself."

He felt a thrill of triumph. As long as he went on being naughty she couldn't ignore him and pet Barbara. He deliberately knocked over the water-jug. She did not know it was done deliberately, but she scolded him for carelessness, and rang for the maid. It took several minutes to wipe it up. Then she turned to Barbara again.

"I'd meant to give you each a penny to spend on the way to school," she said, "but now Jonathan's been so naughty I won't give him one."

Jonathan knew that she had not meant to give them each a penny, that it was a plan formed on the spur of the moment to punish him. He took his piece of bread from his plate and threw it at Barbara, hitting her full in the face. Barbara began to cry, and Rachel turned on him angrily.

"Go away from the table, Jonathan."

He was as angry as she was now. "I won't," he shouted, "I won't, and you can't make me."

She came round to his place and tried to drag him from his chair. He caught hold of the table and struggled, kicking, and shouting.

It was at this point that Frank came in.

"What on earth's the matter?" he said.

He was tired with the morning's work. All he wanted was peace, and, as usual, he came home to a scene.

"It's Jonathan," panted Rachel tempestuously. "I can't do anything with him. He threw his bread at Barbara, and wouldn't go away from the table when I sent him, and——"

Frank dealt with Jonathan shortly and sharply. Jonathan endured his punishment without a tear, but Barbara sobbed more bitterly than ever. She could not bear Jonathan to be punished.

"And now get off to school—both of you," ended Frank.

They went off side by side, Barbara comforted by a sweet that Polly, the maid, popped into her mouth when she saw them off. Jonathan's small person was stinging from his punishment, but there was an odd defiant triumph at his heart. He felt that he was temporarily the victor in that strange, secret, incomprehensible struggle that he waged with his mother.

Frank closed the door and looked at the lunch table. There was a rather unappetising remnant of cold lamb at one end, and a dish of tepid potatoes at the other. The bread had been saturated by water from the overturned water-jug, and the cloth was wet and crumpled.

Considering the effort and time that Rachel spent on her housekeeping, it was remarkably inefficient. He drew his chair to the table, and began to make tentative assaults on the leg of lamb. Then he heard a stifled sound and looked up. His wife had laid her head on her arms on the table, her shoulders heaved convulsively.

"What's the matter?" he said, trying to keep the irritation out of his voice.

"It's Jonathan," she sobbed. "He's been so naughty. He's upset me so."

He schooled himself to speak slowly and patiently.

"Well, my dear, what on earth do you expect? He's only a kid of nine. You might have cause for worry if he behaved like an angel. All kids of his age behave like devils sometimes. It's only natural. He's played the fool and been punished for it. There's nothing to be tragic about."

He had not been able to keep the irritation out of his voice, after all.

She flung up her head and gave him a quick desperate look. Then she pushed her chair back, said, "I'm sorry," in a strangled voice, and went out of the room. He laid down the knife and fork, and sat staring in front of him. Now he'd upset her. He ought to have gone round to her and kissed her and sympathised with her and comforted her. But—these scenes were so incessant. They took place over such trifles.

In spite of his irritation with her, his heart was aching with pity. She tortured herself so exquisitely. She was probably sobbing in desperate misery upstairs now, firmly believing that he hated her just because he had not been sympathetic about Jonathan. He tried hard, but he *couldn't* always be comforting and sympathising and reassuring her. It was like rolling a stone up a hill, a stone that dropped down again the minute you'd got it to the top, it was like trying to fill a sieve with water. You could exhaust every particle of nervous energy you possessed in arguing away her suspicions, teasing away her depression, instilling the subtle drops of flattery that were like wine to her, and then, just as you'd got her happy and cheerful and confident, the veriest trifle would send her down to the depths, and it was all to do over again.

The trouble was that he loved her too much, and understood her too well. She frayed his nerves, and hindered his work, she literally wore him out, but he was as passionately in love with her as he had been when he married her. And she was in love with him. If she had not been, she would not have broken her heart over the least shade of irritation in his manner, and they might both have been happier.

He ate his lunch absently, helping himself to the rice mould and prunes that stood on the dinner waggon against the wall.

When she entered the room again she was composed, but there was something stormy in her very composure, something stormy and infinitely withdrawn.

"I've had proof," she said, "that what you said was quite wrong. I saw Olivia in the town this morning, and she cut me."

"She probably didn't see you."

"Oh yes, she did. . . . I suppose I'm not good enough for Olivia. She's a born snob, you know."

"Is she?"

He knew that Olivia was not a snob, but he felt too much on edge either to defend her or to assent. Sometimes, for the sake of peace, he would agree with Rachel in criticisms of their acquaintances that he knew to be unjust, but he always suffered afterwards from an acute sense of disloyalty.

"And Mrs. Haines cut me, too," went on Rachel, still in a tensely casual voice.

"I'm quite sure she didn't."

"She did. I met her going into Granger's, and she looked at me as if she barely recognised me. Then when I met her again she was going to smile as usual, but I didn't look at her. I like to know where I am with people. People can't know me one minute and not the next."

He felt rather troubled by that. Mrs. Haines was one of his best patients. He attended her and her household regularly. She had asked him to call that afternoon.

He went upstairs to wash his hands, then came down again, took his hat from the hatstand, and stood hesitating at the dining-room door. He knew that she was wretched, that she was longing for his comfort and affection, but he shrank, as usual, from the demands she made on him. He called out: "Well, good-bye, old girl," in an exaggeratedly careless voice, then went quickly down to the gate where his car stood ready for him.

Rachel sat motionless, staring in front of her, wrapped in a black cloud of self-pity. She'd given up everything for her husband, and this was her reward. She'd given up *everything* for him. She worked herself to the bone for him. . . .

She rose tempestuously to her feet and went into the kitchen.

"How long is it since the spare bedroom was done out?" she said to Polly, who sat at the kitchen table with the charwoman, drinking tea and discussing the rival merits of Douglas Fairbanks and Ronald Colman.

"It was done out after Mrs. Morgan had stayed the night," said the girl.

"*Weeks* ago," said Rachel. "I'll do it this after-noon." She took down her overall from a peg in the kitchen. "Get me some hot water."

The two women exchanged glances behind her back. She was in, what they always referred to as, "a state." When she was in "a state", she generally undertook a piece of quite unnecessary work in the house, performing it in a sort of frenzy. It was one of the symptoms.

In a few moments she was engaged in turning out the spare room, setting upon it fiercely, as if it were one of her many imaginary enemies. As she knelt on hands and knees on the bare floor, her sleeves rolled up to the elbows, scrubbing the linoleum, she was two people. One of them was scrubbing the floor of the spare bedroom—working like a slave for the husband who neglected her—the other stood aside and watched with indignant pity. . . .

She remembered that her sister Violet was coming to tea, but she did not hurry over the work on that account. She rather prolonged it. She wanted Violet to find her on her knees scrubbing the spare-room floor like this.

Chapter Eight

VIOLET MORGAN knocked at the front door, and then stood waiting, a smile of anticipatory pleasure on her pretty face. Violet had adored her elder sister from babyhood, and always looked forward eagerly to her weekly visit. The pleasure of the actual visit was seldom commensurate with the pleasure of the anticipation, and she would often return home weighed down by a heavy depression, that she attributed solely to pity for Rachel. Rachel seemed to have more troubles than any one person had a right to expect.

But Rachel in her best mood when things were going well—Rachel care-free, tender, gay—would send Violet home in a radiant glow of happiness. She possessed the optimism of a good, but rather stupid, woman, and, however much Rachel had depressed her one week, her spirits would have risen, and she would think of Rachel as the Rachel of her best mood, when the next week came round.

In her childhood everything that happened to her had seemed incomplete till she had told Rachel about it, and even now, as she stood on the door step, waiting for the door to be opened, she was going over in her mind all the things that she had to tell Rachel this week.

There was the new fur coat that John had bought her, the dance that she and John had gone to last Saturday, the sunk garden that they were making, and, most exciting of all, the Mediterranean cruise that John had decided on for their next holiday. It was a batch of news that would take Rachel right out of herself and cheer her up, if she were feeling depressed. The fact that Rachel and John did not "understand" one another was the greatest sorrow of her life, but she had a pathetic conviction that, if she went on talking to each about the other, they would in time come to see each other as she saw them. Polly opened the door, and she entered with a pleasant smile of greeting.

"Is Mrs. Mainwaring in the drawing-room?"

"No, m'm," said Polly, "she's in the spare room."

Violet told herself that the rather curious look Polly gave her did not mean that Rachel was in a bad mood, but she went upstairs more slowly than she would have gone if Polly had not given it her.

"Hello, darling," she said, as she opened the door.

Rachel rose from her knees, and wiped her steaming hands on her overall. She was hot and tired, and her head was aching. Her energetic turning out of the room had increased rather than lessened the turmoil of her spirit, and the sight of Violet, radiant, cool, expensively dressed, did nothing to soothe it.

"Hello . . . you're rather early, aren't you?"

She smiled as she spoke, but her smile was strained and full of effort, and the blackness of her mood filled the little room as if it were something palpable.

"Am I too early?"

Already some of the eager happiness had faded from the younger sister's face.

"Of course not."

Rachel had untied the apron, and was rolling her sleeves down her red, steaming arms. Violet looked at the pail of water, the scrubbing brush, and dusters.

"Darling," she said, "*need* you do things like that?"

"Of course, I need," said Rachel shortly. "I haven't got a rich husband, and four indoor servants."

There was a faint but unmistakable accent on the 'I.'

"But surely Polly can do this?"

"Polly has other things to do. Come downstairs to the drawing-room. I suppose it's about tea time."

They went downstairs together. Rachel loved her sister. Her jealousy was quite unconscious. Had Violet needed her help, Rachel would have willingly made any sacrifice for her. But Violet did not need her help. That was the trouble. Violet needed nothing. She had everything that a woman could possibly want—beauty, wealth, friends, admiration, an adoring husband. . . . Polly had lit a fire in the drawing-room and set out the tea-table.

"Now, darling," said Violet, drawing up an arm-chair, "you sit down here and rest . . . put your feet up here . . . and I'm going to tell you all my news."

And she began to tell Rachel all her news, talking brightly, vivaciously, in order to cheer her.

Her intentions were excellent, her love of Rachel like a fire in her heart; it was not her fault that she lacked the imagination to realise that the things she told her were just the things most likely to increase her depression.

"The dance was at Lady Crawley's, and she was *so* sweet to me. . . . I danced several times with her brother . . . He's quite a big pot, you know, something or other in the Ministry. . . . Here's the tea. Don't move, darling, I'll pour out . . . you remember that I told you John was going to buy me a fur coat . . . he got me the most gorgeous thing. Mink. I begged him not to get me such an expensive one, but you know how obstinate he is."

The look on Rachel's face could not be ignored any longer.

"What's the matter, darling? Is something worrying you?"

"Oh, only the usual things. Money. The children are always wanting new clothes, and I do so hate bothering Frank. It's a continual struggle to make both ends meet."

Still more of the radiance faded from the younger sister's face.

"Darling," she pleaded, "if only you'd let me *help*——"

Rachel cut her short. "I thought you'd promised me not to mention that again."

"I'm sorry," said Violet unhappily.

Rachel's self-pity was ravenous. It required continual food. And the most satisfying food it could find was the two pictures of herself and Violet, placed side by side—herself: a household drudge, struggling to make both ends meet; Violet: rich, care-free, pampered. To accept gifts from Violet would blur the outline of her picture and make it less satisfying. Rachel, of course, did not realise this. She thought that it was self-respect that made her refuse help from Violet, and it was generally considered "splendid" of her by the family.

"Well, go on telling me your news, Vi."

She spoke in the tone in which one might try to entertain a wearisome child. Violet's assurance had left her. She replied uncertainly, stumblingly.

"Well, nothing much has happened really. . . . Mrs. Campion called yesterday. She was awfully interested in the sunk garden, because they've just been making one."

"She didn't mention me, I suppose?"

"N-no, I don't remember her doing so."

Rachel laughed shortly.

"Oh, she's no use for me nowadays. I haven't got sunk gardens and things to show her."

"Oh, *Rachel!*"

"I'm not being horrid, dear. I'm just stating a fact. I don't mind. She's got time and money for that sort of thing, and I haven't. I don't care for her anyway. I think she's snobbish and insincere. She only makes up to you because of John's money."

"Oh, Rachel, she *is* sincere."

"Well, if you think so, it's all right, isn't it? . . . Now, do tell me what else you've been doing."

But Violet could not tell her any more, though she had not even mentioned the Mediterranean cruise, and she had been looking forward all week to telling Rachel about that.

"I've nothing else. It's your turn to tell me your news. How are the children?"

The children were naughty and troublesome. . . . How was she? She was tired to death all day. . . . How was Frank? He did ten men's work, and got hardly any money, and no gratitude at all. He looked so ill sometimes, that she didn't know how he kept up, but, of course, he had no time to look after himself. . . . How was Polly going on? Polly was so dirty and inefficient that it took more time to look after her than it would take to do the work oneself.

She did most of the work herself in fact. A dreary monotonous recital. . . .

The last glow of the younger sister's radiance had faded. And, as her depression grew, Rachel's seemed strangely to lighten, so that she became almost cheerful, for it gave her an odd perverse satisfaction, that she did not acknowledge or understand, to strip Violet of her confidence and happiness, to make her share, if even for a short time, the black cloud that enveloped herself.

But her cheerfulness was short-lived. As soon as Violet had gone, her depression sprang upon her again, like a beast from ambush. She went slowly and draggingly upstairs to say good night to the children. Barbara was only half awake. She kissed her with warm sleepy lips, and murmured that Brenda's measles were better. Brenda was Barbara's doll, who was continually ill with the various diseases that she heard Frank mention.

"I'm so glad, darling," said Rachel, as she tucked her up.

Then she went on to Jonathan, and kissed him wearily. She was so tired and dispirited that she had given up the fight for possession of him. It was a truce in their warfare. He sensed her relaxing of the struggle, and abandoned himself to his love for her, clinging to her tightly. He could let himself love her, when she was not fighting him for himself. Yet, even as he clung to her, he was on the alert, ready to withdraw himself at the least sign of her renewal of the conflict. But she did not renew it. She lay with him in silence on his bed, her arms round him, and his round her. Then she arose slowly, as if with an effort, said "Good night, darling," tucked him up, and went very quietly away.

He lay in bed, feeling happy and at peace. It was so nice when people loved you, and yet let you belong to yourself, instead of wanting to know the things you thought and felt, just as if those things belonged to anyone but yourself, instead of asking you questions that they had no right to ask you, and then saying you were "rude" if you didn't answer. Gran hadn't been like that. She never wanted to come any further into yourself than you invited her, and when you told her about yourself, she told you about herself in exchange. She didn't think you couldn't understand. She told him that she'd cried when Sally, her little dog, was run over, and no one else in the world, not even Grandad, knew that. He had been terribly, terribly sorry when Gran died. He always thought of her in bed before he went to sleep.

Frank was rather silent during the evening. He had visited Mrs. Haines in the afternoon, and her manner to him had been distant and constrained. Usually she was friendliness itself. It was obvious that Rachel had offended her. He did not mention it till they were going to bed: then he said suddenly:

"I say, old girl."

"Yes."

"You honestly ought to be more careful how you behave to people."

Rachel swung round from the dressing-table and fixed tragic, dilated eyes on him.

"What do you mean?"

"Mrs. Haines. I went to see her this afternoon, and it was quite evident that she was annoyed by what happened this morning. She's a good patient, and it will make a lot of difference to me if I lose her."

Her eyes, still fixed on him, seemed to grow yet bigger and darker. She was going to take the thing in an exaggerated way as she took everything, of course, and make a scene over it. Well, he hated scenes but she must understand that she couldn't go about the town cutting his best patients.

"I didn't understand. I'll write and apologise," she said, breathlessly.

"Of course you mustn't. That'll only make it worse."

"I'll go and see her."

"Don't be so absurd."

"What can I do?"

"You can't do anything now. The harm's done."

It was the culmination of the whole hateful day. The frail barrier of her self-control broke down.

"What on earth's the matter?"

She answered him through desperate, strangled sobs. "I've never been any use to anyone, and now I've ruined your career, and you hate me, and I wish I was dead."

He came across to the bed and gathered her in his arms, comforting her, stroking back her hair, kissing her tear-stained cheeks, her red quivering lips. All his irritation with her was merged in a flood of passionate love and pity. The tempest of her emotion gradually spent itself, but he still held her in his arms, straining her to him, his lips pressed against hers.

Chapter Nine

IT was always a scramble for Joy and Miss Nash to get the children ready for breakfast. Miss Nash, Joy's mother's help, was a tall, thin woman, whose disproportionately small head, poised on a long neck, gave her rather an odd appearance. She had an unfailing fund of cheerfulness, an unbounded capacity for hard work, and no existence at all outside the affairs of the Ranger family. When Dickie won the Never-late-never-absent prize, Miss Nash felt as most people feel only when they have backed the winner of the Derby. When Laura asked one of her delicious questions ("Is God an angel or a fairy?"), Miss Nash would write to all her friends and relations in order to tell them about it. Joy sometimes had to discourage her from repeating to the visitors who came to the house every remark that any of the children had ever made. Miss Nash kept a diary of their sayings and doings, and would refresh her memory when visitors were expected. Just as a missionary feels bound to preach the tenets of his faith, so Miss Nash felt impelled to prove to everyone what wonderful children were Dickie and Billy and Laura and Bobs. They were often shy when people came to tea, and did not do themselves justice, so Miss Nash had to do them justice instead. Miss Nash had a vague and shadowy family-circle of her own in the background that existed, in Miss Nash's eyes, only as an audience for the sayings and doings of the little Rangers. It is perhaps unnecessary to add that Miss Nash's family-circle received Miss Nash's eulogies of the little Rangers without even a pretence of sympathy.

Miss Nash was helping Dickie and Billy, aged eight and six, to dress. Joy was dressing Laura, who was four, and trying to reassure

Bobs, who, with all the strength of her eighteen-months'-old lungs, was clamorously demanding to be dressed too. Between the stages of Laura's dressing, Joy was flying up and down the stairs to make sure that the daily woman had arrived and was getting the breakfast ready without burning the toast or over-boiling the eggs. Joy, in fact, seemed to be everywhere at once. Her voice was heard first in her bedroom, then on the landing, then on the stairs, then in the kitchen, and then back again on the landing.

"Yes, precious. Mummy will dress you in a moment. Very well, Laura. Put them on yourself, but just let Mummy help a bit. This little leg in this little hole, and this. . . . Mrs. Marret, the toast's burning, I can smell it. . . . Oh, and don't use any of yesterday's milk. It turned; I meant to throw it away. Yes, Mummy's coming, darling. . . . Dickie, don't shout so. I can't hear a word Mrs. Marret says. . . . Yes, there is some more butter. It's in the meat safe. . . . Miss Nash, be sure they clean their teeth, won't you? Billy didn't yesterday. No, sweetheart, you've got them on wrong. Just let Mummy help. . . . The eggs have been on long enough, Mrs. Marret, I'm sure. . . . Yes, what a clever boy. . . . Mummy's coming in a minute, Bobs darling . . . and this little arm through this little hole and . . . Yes, Bruce, in the left-hand drawer. . . . I know they're there, dear, if you look. . . . Dickie *darling*, don't shout so. . . . Yes, sing but don't shout. . . . Well, tell him he mustn't. Billy, you mustn't eat the tooth-paste. Take it from him, Miss Nash. Yes, darling, you dressed yourself all by yourself. What a clever girlie! Now just help Mummy with Bobs. Give me her things from the chair. . . . such a helpful little girl. All right, treasure, she's going to be dressed now. But, Bruce, I *said* the left-hand drawer. . . . Yes, Billy, you can jump high, but go back to Miss Nash, darling, because we're all so busy in here. Oh, *darling!* Mrs. Marret, will you come and wipe up some water? Laura's knocked the jug over."

They were all ready at last in the dining-room, and Joy was bustling round the table, tying on feeders, pouring out milk, spreading pieces of bread and butter with coverings of egg. Miss Nash's especial charge at meal time was Laura, and Joy's was Bobs, who sat next to her in her high chair. Bruce sat at the head of the table, eating his breakfast with one eye on the clock, and occasionally murmuring: "Quietly, old chap," or, "All right, old man, I'm listening," and smiling across the table at Bobs, whom he adored, and saying, "Where's Daddy's baby?" to which she always replied by pointing to herself, and saying with a grin, "He 't is."

There was a deep peace and radiant happiness in Joy's heart. She clung to it desperately, knowing how soon it was to be shattered.

"Well, Mummy," said Bruce, "time I was off."

She looked up at him. In addition to his plainness there was something clumsily common about him. He had not, she knew, a single original idea of any sort. His conversation consisted entirely of comments on items of news from the cheap papers that were his sole reading. ("How dreadful about this murder in Peckham. . . ." "I see that Medham's resigning." . . . "I'm afraid there's going to be more trouble in India.")

But he was kind and honest and unselfish, and she loved him with a sort of yearning tenderness that filled every corner of her being. She could forgive any injury to herself, but she could not forgive the most tenuous slight to Bruce. Even now she carried in her heart something of the bitter resentment she had felt when first she realised the contempt that underlay her father's pleasant manner to him. She had never forgiven Christopher for that. It had been the end of their old friendship. She was so sensitive on Bruce's behalf that she saw shadows of that contempt everywhere, saw it in Olivia's weary remoteness, in Derek's patronising boisterousness, in Frank's quiet twinkle. Bruce was worth ten thousand of them, she told herself indignantly. All his thought and care were for her and the children. He hated to spend money on himself. He lunched on bread and cheese, and wore his clothes till they were dropping to pieces. He would often go without cigarettes in order to bring home little presents for her and the children. And Derek and Olivia, in their smug prosperity, looked down on him: Frank watched him with that hateful twinkle in his eyes. . . .

"How did the old man seem last night?" said Bruce.

"I thought he was splendid," said Joy. She spoke rather more emphatically than was necessary. A sudden memory had come to her, slipping under her guard. An old man, bewildered, lonely, rather frightened. She shut her eyes to it quickly, and, when she opened them, she had changed the picture so that it made no claims on her.

"He's got over it wonderfully well," she went on. "Of course, he's always been fond of reading, and going for long walks. Now that the shock's over he's settling down splendidly."

"He must miss your mother," said Bruce.

Suppose she died, she thought, and Bruce was left alone. . . . Suppose Bruce died, and she was left alone. But that was different. . . . No two people in the world felt for each other as she and Bruce felt.

"I expect he's a bit lonely," continued Bruce.

"Yes," she said breathlessly, "but, when people get to that age, I suppose they begin to take for granted that one of them will be left without the other."

They took it for granted, of course. It didn't make them unhappy. Old people were placid and resigned. Nothing made them unhappy.

Laura was being difficult about her breakfast, lying back in her chair, and refusing to eat it. Miss Nash, kindly, vivacious, and persuasive, was making up a ridiculous tale, in which the little squares of honey-sandwich were rash intruders into an ogre's castle, which was Laura's mouth.

"And he never came home, so the next brother said, 'I'll go and see what's happened to him,' so he climbed the mountain to the cave (the dice of sandwich paused outside Laura's little red mouth, that was trying to pout, but couldn't help smiling), and said, 'Open, Sesame,' and the cave slowly opened (Laura obviously didn't want to open her mouth, but as obviously couldn't resist doing it), and he went in, and the cave slowly closed on him (Laura's red lips closed), and the ogre's cooks began to cut him up (Laura's little teeth began to chew energetically), and then they sent him down the red staircase for the ogre (Laura swallowed slowly and importantly). Well, he never came home; so his next brother. . . ."

Joy tried not to feel irritated by Miss Nash's high-pitched emphatic voice. She was so wonderful with the children, but she did get so

57

unbearably on one's nerves. (A placid, resigned, quite happy, old man—not bewildered, or lonely, or unhappy—reading and going for long walks.)

Bruce had risen, and was leaning over her to kiss her.

"Goodbye, darling," he said.

"Goodbye. Come back soon as you can."

He never stayed away from his home a second longer than he had to, but he would have felt vaguely disappointed if she had not said that to him when he went to work in the morning.

Joy stood at the dining-room window, and waved to him as he turned to shut the gate. Then he disappeared, and the anxiety that was her daily companion raised its head in her heart. She went on giving Bobs her breakfast, but all the peace and happiness had left her. She saw Bruce knocked down by taxis, run over by trams, crushed by falling lifts, or, if he reached the office safely, jeered at by the younger clerks, bullied by his employer.

Miss Nash was getting the three elder children ready for school. She was exultantly self-gratulatory over her victory in the matter of Laura's breakfast.

"I don't think the little monkey would have eaten a crumb if I hadn't made up that ridiculous story."

"You're wonderful, Miss Nash," said Joy rather wearily.

If only the woman would be wonderful, she thought, without having to be perpetually told that she was wonderful. . . .

Miss Nash's exultation was short-lived, however, for Laura was suddenly stricken with remorse at having eaten the thirty-four brothers, and sobbingly demanded that they should be taken out of her at once, and restored to their mother.

Miss Nash pretended to do this, but Laura refused to be satisfied, and Joy had to say, "Now that's enough, Laura," in her firmest tones, before Laura could be persuaded to let Miss Nash get her ready for school.

Miss Nash always took them to school. Billy was eight, and wore a pale blue cap and pale blue tops to his stockings, and went to a prep. school. He thought it babyish to be taken to school, and always made Miss Nash leave him at the end of the road in which his school was. While pretending to go away, she always loitered about watching him furtively till he was safely within the gates.

At home Joy began to tidy up after the children and Miss Nash. That was the worst of Miss Nash. She was not methodical, and someone always had to tidy up after her. When she had got the children ready for school, you found button-hooks on the floor, hair-brushes on chairs, towels over chair-backs, and toys everywhere. When Joy spoke to her about it, she was so surprised and remorseful ("I'm *so* sorry, Mrs. Ranger, I simply can't *think* how I came to do a thing like that. It's the sort of thing I *never* do, as a rule. I'm generally so *careful* to clear everything up. . . ."), that it was less trouble to tidy up after her, and say nothing about it. Sometimes, when Miss Nash had been particularly irritating and particularly untidy, Joy played with the idea of getting rid of her, but she knew really that she would never get anyone else who loved the children as Miss Nash loved them, who would cheerfully do the daily woman's work when she failed them, who did not want any holidays (Miss Nash could hardly be persuaded to take her official "afternoon"), who, in fact, had no life at all outside the little family.

Joy went upstairs to make her bed, preceded slowly and importantly by Bobs, who pulled herself up with both hands on to each step refusing to be helped.

There were times when Joy lived in a kind of waking nightmare, in which imaginary people dealt imaginary unkindnesses to Bobs. She, Joy, died, and Bruce's second wife didn't like Bobs, and was unkind to her. Joy expended a good deal of hatred upon Bruce's second wife.

At the sound of Miss Nash's return, Joy's anxieties hastily readjusted themselves. The children had escaped all the dangers that lurked in the streets. They were safe. . . . But, of course, it was only a relative safety. The whistling sound of the wind outside sent her thoughts to Billy's weak chest. Not a single spring of Billy's life had gone by without his having bronchitis, and he had had pneumonia twice. His desk was probably under an open window (she had written to ask them not to put his desk in a draughty spot, but they never took any notice of letters, and they hated parents who "fussed"). He would go out at "break" into the playground, and, even if he remembered to put on his coat, he would stand about in a draught and get his cough worse. He looked so sturdy and rosy-cheeked that people could not believe that he was delicate. He had been terribly ill last spring. As she finished making the beds and tidying the bedrooms, her thoughts were hovering about Billy, guarding him, protecting him, devastating with her hatred the people who let him sit under open windows, who let him go out without his coat, who let him stand about in draughts. . . .

Miss Nash came into the bedroom, lifting up Bobs, who was busily engaged in scribbling over the pages of a tradesman's catalogue on the hearthrug.

"Well, how's the darling?" she said in her rather shrill voice.

Bobs wrinkled up her delicious little nose in a smile of welcome.

"Left them all safely?" said Joy, smoothing the counterpane.

"Oh yes," said Miss Nash, and added proudly, "Miss Golding said that Laura had painted a nice flower yesterday."

That slightly—very slightly—eased the dragging anxiety about Laura and Miss Golding.

It was Miss Golding's head mistress who had persuaded Joy to send Laura to the new "nursery class" that she was just forming, and of which Miss Golding was to be the teacher. Joy had thought Miss Golding charming when she went to the school to make the arrangements. But, when she took Laura there at the beginning of this term, she had seemed quite different. She had said:

"Oh yes, I remember. Laura's her name, isn't it? Sit here, Laura. She'll be quite all right, Mrs. Ranger. You can leave her now."

And, just as Joy was turning reluctantly to leave Laura, a stranger in a strange land, a little girl had come up to Miss Golding's desk and said: "Do look what I found yesterday, Miss Golding," and Miss Golding has said: "Go and sit down, and don't bother me now." The words, of course, were nothing, but the sudden sharpness of the tone sent Joy's heart racing unevenly. If it had not been too late, she would have taken Laura away at once. She went home, and spent the rest of the morning composing letters to the head mistress in which she withdrew Laura from the school, and gave various unconvincing reasons for her sudden decision.

Then Laura had come home, covered with coloured chalk, intensely pleased with herself, and full of excitement at the thought of going to school again to-morrow. So Joy had never written the letter, and Laura trotted off to school every morning with Miss Nash. Laura seemed happy there, but, of course, one could never be quite sure. Children were so inarticulate. . . . And whenever Laura seemed tired on her return from school, whenever she seemed to set off reluctantly with Miss Nash in the morning, Joy felt again this agonised indignation, this tense fierce hatred of Miss Golding.

"Miss Golding was quite pleasant?" she said to Miss Nash with exaggerated carelessness.

Miss Nash did not know—no one knew, not even Bruce—the torment of anxiety that was Joy's daily bread. Miss Nash thought that there were no more wonderful children in the world than the little Rangers, but she never suffered any anxiety on their behalf. Joy, on the other hand, knew that there was nothing wonderful about them, but she was tortured by anxiety for them every minute of every day.

"Oh, yes, I think she's charming," said Miss Nash, "and she takes such an interest in Laura. Of course, I honestly do believe that Laura has great artistic talent."

Joy laughed happily. Miss Golding was evidently in a good temper this morning.

"Nonsense," she said. "You know that you didn't know whether the last thing she brought home was a sunflower or a goldfish."

"It was very cleverly done in any case," said Miss Nash stoutly.

Joy still felt light-hearted with relief, as she got Bobs ready to go into the town to buy a new pair of shoes.

Bobs loved getting her new shoes. She smiled at the shop assistant and patted his head, crooning "Man" over him affectionately, when he knelt down to try them on. She carried the parcel back to her pram herself, then went soundly to sleep as soon as Joy had lifted her into it. Joy found the sunny keenness of the day exhilarating, and her spirits rose, to drop suddenly, as she encountered a fierce East wind that sent her thoughts to Billy. At the corner of the High Street, she came upon Dr. Lethbridge. He smiled at her and drew up his grey battleship of a car. He had been their friend from childhood, and the sight of his rugged face and shaggy beard always vaguely reassured her. When he smiled at her like that she felt confident that Billy was not going to have bronchitis again.

"That Bobs?" He bent down to look into the pram at the sleeping baby. "She gets bonnier every time I see her. She's a credit to us, isn't she?"

"Bruce and I think she's perfect," smiled Joy.

"The others all right?"

"Yes. Billy's got a little cough."

"The monkey! He would have. . . . I suppose you saw your father last night? What did you think of him?"

"I thought he was looking splendid, considering."

"Considering, yes. He's had a terrible shock, you know. It's worse for him than it would be for a lot of men. Your mother was an exceptionally charming woman. . . . Well, I mustn't waste my time."

He raised his hat, the battleship roared, then sailed slowly down the street.

Joy walked on thoughtfully. It seemed strange to hear Mother spoken of as an exceptionally charming woman. To Joy she had just been Mother—the person who looked after one, and comforted one, and bought one's clothes when one was little, and who, later, arranged parties for one, but kept more in the background, and who, later still, had the children to tea, and bought them things that one could not have afforded to buy oneself. "An exceptionally charming woman." . . . No, Joy could never see her like that. To Joy she had just been Mother, and then Granny, and that was all. . . .

She was passing Dickie's school now. It stood by itself in a large garden, hidden from the road by trees. It thrilled her to think of Dickie there, his tousled head bent over his desk, his blue eyes frowning at his books. Thrilled her and—— Sometimes she tried not to think of it, but it was always there, waiting at the back of her mind. It had happened several months ago. She had been tidying Dickie's drawers, and had come across a toy monkey, about two inches high, that she had never seen before. Dickie could not have bought it, because she knew exactly how he had spent his pocket money every week. If someone had given it to him, surely he would have told her. . . . She called him up, and asked where it had come from. He said that he had found it in the road that morning. But he flushed as he said it, and his blue eyes shifted from hers. She got it out of him at last. He had taken it from a shop. He defended himself vehemently.

"But I wanted it, Mummy, and I hadn't any money, and there were hundreds of them. The man would never miss it, and no one saw me take it."

Horrified and bewildered, she tried to reason with him. It belonged to the man, she said. It was stealing to take it.

"But, Mummy, I told you he had *hundreds* of others. He wouldn't miss one. I wouldn't have taken it if he hadn't had a lot more."

"Suppose other people took your things just because they wanted them."

"I shouldn't mind if I'd got *hundreds* of them like the man," he said.

"Suppose everyone took things out of shops just because they wanted them."

"But they don't, Mummy. And he'd never miss *one*."

"Suppose the man went and told the police that you'd taken it."

"But he didn't see me, Mummy. He doesn't know I've got it, so he won't mind if he doesn't know."

Would he take her things, and Billy's, and Laura's, and Bobs's, she asked, just because he wanted them?

"I would if you had hundreds and hundreds of one thing like him. . . . I'd *know* you wouldn't mind."

Why didn't he ask the man, then, if he thought he wouldn't mind?

"I thought he might say 'no,' Mummy, but, if I took it, he wouldn't know about it, and I wanted it so terribly."

"Why didn't you tell me that you'd taken it?"

"I thought you might be cross. Mummy."

"Then you knew it was wrong?"

"No, but I thought you mightn't understand."

She tried to explain to him exactly why stealing was wrong, and, when it came to the point, found that she was not quite sure herself.

"But I wouldn't mind anyone taking my things, Mummy, if I'd got hundreds of them like he had. ... Yes, but they only cost threepence, and he looked a rich man. ... But, Mummy, I *knew* he'd got enough money to buy his children food without that threepence. ... Yes, but everyone else *wasn't* taking them."

So she began to tell him about little boys who had been sent to reformatories, and men who had been sent to prison. That frightened him, and she hated herself for frightening him. In the end, he sobbed and clung to her, and said that he'd *kill* himself if a policeman tried to take him away from her. She took him down to the shop to confess to the shopman, and give back the monkey. His eyes were red and swollen. He looked a pathetic little object. The shopman was very kind to him, and looked at Joy reproachfully, as if thinking that she had been too hard on him. On their way home they passed a policeman, and Dickie clutched her hand convulsively. Bruce went up to his room to talk to him that night when he came home, but Dickie hardly listened to what he said. He was sitting up in bed, his bright eyes fixed on the door.

"If they try to take me away," he said, when Bruce had finished talking, "I'll fight, and fight, and *fight*. I don't care if they kill me, I won't let them take me away from you and Mummy."

It ended by their consoling him, and assuring him that no one would take him away, but he woke up screaming five or six times in the night. The next day he refused to go out, because a policeman was walking up and down the road, and when at last they persuaded him to go out, he was sick in the road as soon as he had passed the policeman. He had nightmare for several nights afterwards, and then he seemed to forget all about it.

Joy was miserable. It was evident that she had tackled the affair on the wrong lines, but she did not know how else she could have tackled it. She never mentioned the matter to him again, and she thought that he had completely forgotten it. Secretly she lived in terror. She searched his drawers when he was at school, she kept a careful check of his pocket money. Once, when the head master sent a message asking her to call and see him, she felt so shaken that she could hardly walk up to the school. But the head master had not wanted to tell her that Dickie was stealing money. He only wanted to know if she would allow him join a carpentering class that was being started at half term. Still Joy's anxiety could never rest, and many times a day, in imagination, she would live through Dickie's expulsion from a public school, through his being sent to a reformatory, through his being sentenced to a long term of imprisonment for embezzlement.

Then, just as she was with Dickie in prison, she met Olivia. Generally she avoided Olivia, because Olivia was poised and aloof, as if troubles and worries could never touch her. She always felt, too, that Olivia and Derek looked down on Bruce, because Bruce was only a managing-clerk, and Derek was head of a large and prosperous business. But just now she was glad to meet her, because it banished the picture of Dickie in prison.

They stood there talking, and, as they did so, the memory of Olivia's two babies came to Joy suddenly, bringing a pang that she dismissed quickly, telling herself, as she always told herself, that Olivia had not cared, had not even wanted children. No one had ever heard her say a single word of regret. You could tell by the way she ignored Bobs now that she did not care for children. No one who cared for children in the very least could have resisted looking at Bobs.

As she hurried homeward, her thoughts went back to Bruce, remorseful for having neglected him so long, forming an armour round him, so that his employer's unkindness could not hurt him, so that the buses and lorries and all the other things intent on his destruction should be powerless against him.

In the afternoon, Miss Nash went out with Bobs, and Joy took

Laura to her dancing class. As she sat with the other mothers, her eyes fixed absently on the tiny figures pirouetting in the big hall, her mind was engaged on functions that she euphemistically termed her "prayers". They were in reality imperious orders issued to the Deity. ("Take care of him; don't let Mr. Dawes be unkind to him; keep Dickie good; take care of Bobs and Miss Nash, when they get to the crossing at the market place—there isn't always a policeman there. . . .")

Sometimes these orders were accompanied by menaces. ("If you let anything happen to them, I'll never believe in you again, and I'll never go to church.") Sometimes by coaxing. ("If you'll look after them, I'll never forget my prayers, and I'll always take the children to church.")

When the dancing class was over, she bundled Laura into her coat, and took her home to tea. Dickie was late, and she passed an agonised quarter of an hour, furtively making sure that the water was hot and that there were plenty of bandages ready in case he had had an accident. He came home, singing merrily, in time for tea. The evening was the usual breathless rush. As soon as tea was over, it was time to put Bobs to bed, then it was time to put Laura to bed, and then the boys. Then there was the dinner to see to, and then Bruce came home. He brought her a big box of chocolates, a present from Mr. Dawes, his employer. He had called at Woolworth's to buy a cloth donkey for Bobs.

Joy accepted her chocolates with a pretence of pleasure (because it would have hurt Bruce if she had not done so), but with secret indignation. Mr. Dawes only sent her chocolates when he had been particularly disagreeable to Bruce the day before, and was feeling a little ashamed of himself. Joy let the children eat the chocolates, but she never touched them herself. After dinner she sat with Bruce by the fire in the dining-room, while Miss Nash washed up. A blissful languor of happiness stole over her, a blessed, blessed ecstasy of content. They were all safe at home under her wing—the babies warm and asleep upstairs, Bruce smoking by the fire with his evening paper. No harm could come to them now. They were safe until to-morrow took them away from her again into danger.

She closed her eyes and leant back in her chair. The day had been long and strenuous. She had languished in prison with them; she had watched by their death beds; she had seen them ill-treated and persecuted. It had been very tiring, and it was all to do again to-morrow.

But, as she sat there wearily relaxed in her chair, she felt a sudden exultant pity for all the women in the world who had not Bruce for a husband, and for children Dickie and Billy and Laura and Bobs.

Chapter Ten

OLIVIA moved restlessly about the drawing-room, straightening cushions and ornaments with nervous mechanical movements. Passing the lacquered mirror that hung between the framed Chinese embroideries on the wall, she threw a quick searching glance at her reflection. As a sort of challenge to fate, she had taken no pains over her appearance in preparation for Stephen's visit. She had not even changed into an afternoon dress, as she would have done if she had not been expecting him. She still wore the plain jersey suit that she had worn in the morning—a suit of a dull red shade that she had never cared for. Her face was pale, and she had used neither rouge nor powder. It was as if she said: "This is I. I'm plain and unattractive. Don't love me. It will really be simpler for all of us if you don't love me."

Stephen Arnold was Ravenham's foremost solicitor. His visits to her had, at first, been professional. He managed the estate of her grandfather, of which she had a twentieth share—thirty pounds a year—and several months ago her consent had been needed for some alterations in the investments. The professional need for his visits had ceased, but his visits continued. Olivia was not introspective or analytical, and she had not realised that she was falling in love with him till it was too late to stop herself. She had known, for some time, that she looked forward eagerly to his visits, that she felt a strange, unreasoning happiness whenever he was near her, but it was not till yesterday that she had realised, suddenly and definitely, what this meant. She had lain awake all night wondering what she ought to do, and the decision she had come to was that she must put an end to their friendship.

If he suggested another meeting this afternoon, she must hesitate, and try to make him think that she was tired of his visits. When next he rang her up to ask if he might call, she must say that she was going out.

There came the sound of his quiet, pleasant voice in the hall. Her heart quickened, and she forgot everything in the world but the fact that he was near her. He entered, his hands outstretched. "Well, how are you?"

He was tall, lean, stooping. When first she met him she had thought that he would have been good-looking had his cheeks been less hollowed, and his sensitive mobile lips less long. He was neither smart nor well groomed, but there was about his figure something vaguely suggestive of elegance, that Ravenham generally described as "distinguished looking".

She put her hands in his, and her eyes returned his smile. She was thinking how strange it was that sometimes, when she tried to recall his features, though she might have seen him only the day before, the memory of them refused to come back to her. Curiously, it was his hands that she could always remember—thin hands, with prominent veins, and long slender fingers.

"Tell me about everything," he went on. "I hear that your father-in-law's home again. How is he?"

Their conversation had never gone beyond superficialities. It surprised her sometimes to realise how slight and conventional had been their acquaintance, judged by the number of times they had met, and the words that had actually passed between them. Their knowledge of each other seemed to have its roots in something so deep that there was no need of words.

"It's aged him terribly," she was saying. "They were inseparable, you know."

"I know. I was at the funeral. He looked absolutely broken up then. I haven't seen him since he came back, of course."

"I think he's better. He looks terribly old still. We all went in last night to see him. He's picking up the threads again, or rather I suppose he's making the best of the life that's left him. He always hated doing anything without her."

The interest and sympathy of her tone were mechanical. Christopher didn't matter. He was an old man. His life was over. He wasn't real. Only she and Stephen were real.

"Poor old chap!" said Stephen, reflectively. "They were the old-fashioned Darby and Joan couple."

Olivia's impatience with Christopher became strangely tinged with jealousy. What claim had he on their pity? He had had a long and happy life with Derek's mother. Their love had lasted serene and unclouded till her death. It was envy, not pity, he deserved.

"The worst is over for him," she said.

"I suppose so," said Stephen.

Like hers, his interest in the old man was perfunctory. He was looking at her, as if trying to fix in his memory for ever the transparent alabaster of her skin, the dark vividness of eyes and hair. As he looked at her the torment of his love swept over him, and he felt the sudden blind panic of something trapped. She passed him his teacup with a faint smile. Her heart was beating unevenly. It was the first time that the mysterious something that united them had threatened to rise to the surface, to rend the tissues of their superficial relationship. But, of course, it was inevitable. It had to happen. It had to be faced. The miracle was that it had not happened sooner.

"And how are things going with you?" she said, trying to speak casually.

"Splendidly. I had a marvellous find the other day. A Queen Anne card-table going really cheap."

"Where have you put it?"

"In the alcove near the fireplace in the study. It's been crying out for it for years. I put it there, then stood and looked at it, and preened myself, till suddenly it occurred to me that what I felt was just what a sparrow feels when he finds a nice feather for his nest."

"Of course," she laughed, "but why should you mind that?"

"I didn't, but it made me feel chastened somehow. As a matter of fact, though, it's rather nice. You must come and see it."

There was a constrained silence, and a faint colour crept into her cheeks. She knew and loved the study where he kept his treasures, and spent most of his time, but she hated the rest of his house, hated inexpressibly the smart, vivacious woman who was his wife.

He rose and went over to the window. Her eyes followed him furtively, studying his face. His thin straight lips ended uncertainly, ready to curve upwards in humour, or grimly downwards. It was his eyes that seemed to show the real man, gentle, kind, honest, understanding.

"Your gardener," he said, "looks an embittered man."

"He is," she said, joining him at the window. "He had a Union Jack tattooed on each wrist during the war."

"But why should that embitter him?"

"Because he joined the Communists since, and, of course, he can't un-tattoo the Union Jack. It's *so* trying for him."

"It must be," he agreed. "In appearance he's like a man who used to run the Band of Hope in my childhood."

She laughed.

"Sit down and have a cigarette. . . . Tell me about him."

He lit her cigarette, then his. "He used to hold classes once a week. We were all sent to them by our parents. We learnt to draw pictures of the stomach—beautifully pear-shaped, and elaborately coloured—before, and after, habitual indulgence in alcohol. I don't think that it occurred to him as inconsistent that, in the room where we had the lessons, there was a large engraving of the Miracle of Cana in Galilee. Probably he'd persuaded himself that the Bible account was incorrect, and that it was the wine that was turned into water, not the water into wine."

She still had the sensation of fighting off something. They must go on talking like this, so that the thing that was threatening them could not come nearer.

"Tell me more about him," she said breathlessly.

"He used to recite at all the local concerts. He had a set of actions that he used for every verse, irrespective of the words. He began by stretching his arms straight before him, then he drew his right arm to his heart, then he threw out both arms on a level with his body, then he dropped them to his side. He had a quivering emotional intonation, without any variation, and he always used just these four movements. I've heard him recite 'The Wreck of the Hesperus', and 'The Glory of the Garden' (they were both favourites of his), with exactly the same intonation and action. He was much in demand as a reciter, and was considered very talented."

"It sounds delightful," she smiled. "I wish I'd known you then."

"I wish you had."

She caught her breath, and looked away from him. The thing was so near now, that it seemed as if it could not be avoided. Yet she made another almost superhuman effort.

"How's Clarissa?" she said.

It was successful. The thing drew away again. The corners of his long mouth softened into a smile of brooding tenderness.

"She's marvellous," he said. "We went for a walk on Sunday afternoon, and saw the most unsavoury-looking tramp you can imagine, eating bread and cheese by the roadside. She said, 'Oh, do look, Daddy, there's a gentleman having a picnic all by himself.' She seemed to think he was very selfish not to share the fun. She'd have joined him for two pins."

"You and she generally go for a walk on Sunday, don't you?"

"Yes, we take the bus out to Henton Common, and start our walk from there. We go through Beltham Woods on tiptoe, without speaking, because Clarissa says that the fairies are asleep there on Sunday afternoon, and if we pick flowers we pick the whole of a group together, because they don't like being separated from their friends. She's very particular about that."

She loved Stephen's little girl with something of the love that should have belonged to her own children, but there was a subtle poison of unconscious jealousy at her heart, as if the child were her rival.

"She's six now, isn't she?" she asked. "What are you going to do with her?"

"About school, you mean? We're already fighting about it. Wanda wants a boarding school, and I don't."

At the mention of his wife the atmosphere had grown tense again. Both were silent. Then,

"I'd better not come again, had I?" he said, quietly.

They had never admitted their love by word or deed, but it lay at last in the open between them. Neither thought of denying it.

She gave a little strangled sob. "You mustn't leave me," she said. "I couldn't bear it."

The barriers were down. His arms were about her, his lips upon hers. At the touch of his body an ecstasy unknown before possessed her.

"I wish we could die like this now," she cried.

"Don't, don't!"

"What are we going to do?"

"I don't know. I can't think. I love you so."

"It's come so suddenly. I didn't know——"

"I knew. I knew all along."

"What are we going to do?"

"I don't know. Kiss me again."

Suddenly through the silence of the room came the sound of a key turning in the lock.

"Derek!" she whispered.

He released her, and she went quickly over to the looking-glass. It surprised her that there were tears on her cheeks. She did not know that she had been crying. She wiped away the traces of them and straightened her hair. When Derek came in she was sitting by the tea-table, and Stephen was standing by the window. There was a bright colour in her cheeks. She wished it had not happened just then, just like that: that she had not had to leave Stephen's arms at the sound of her husband's key in the lock. It seemed to cheapen and debase their love.

Stephen looked white and strained, but Derek never noticed what people looked like. He took the cup of tea that Olivia poured out, and began to talk to Stephen, "holding forth" as he loved to, ignoring comments and interruptions. Other people existed to Derek only as admirers of his personality, and audiences of his views. They had no distinct or separate individualities. When they made any contribution to the conversation, he waited politely till they had finished, and then went on at the point where he had been before they broke in. As he talked, he was the Image, handsome, charming, brilliant. He saw Stephen only as a potential worshipper of the Image.

"We probably shan't be in this house much longer. It's too ridiculously small. I've been considering Merton Towers. That's more the sort of thing I want."

Stephen rose with an abrupt, jerky movement, interrupting the monologue. The compression of his lips deepened the furrows in his cheeks, making him look almost haggard.

"Well. . . . I must be off."

Derek accompanied him to the front door, still talking vivaciously.

When he came back to the drawing-room, the familiar expression of ill-humour had returned to his handsome face. He threw himself into a chair, and sat there huddled, scowling viciously in front of him.

His business was losing ground daily. Firms that had dealt with him for years were leaving him. And all his fear, all his anger, all his misery were concentrated in a deep sense of injury against his wife. He had to blame someone for the morass in which he found himself, and she was the easiest person to blame. Ignoring the fact that he had resented any inquiries about his affairs as interference, he told himself now that she went her easy way, with never a word or look of sympathy, never the slightest effort to help, never even an inquiry as to how things were going with him. It was all her fault. It was her extravagance that had ruined him, not his own incompetence. He sat upright and began to look about the room for something that his smouldering anger could seize upon.

"That dress of yours is new, isn't it?" he rapped out viciously.

"I don't know what you think I've bought it with, if it is," she said quietly. "I've had the utmost difficulty in getting money from you to pay the bills, and I think you know that I've had to use my own money for housekeeping." A sudden gust of anger against him seized her, and she ended unsteadily, "I do all I can to help you, and I'm sick of your behaving like this, Derek."

Her indirect reference to his financial straits had infuriated him. He turned on her, white and snarling.

"All right, if you're sick of me, go. Put on your things, and get out. Go to hell."

He flung out of the room.

She sat tense and trembling. Her anger and his had shaken her. Then the tenseness left her. Her body relaxed, and her eyes grew soft and dreamy. . . . She did not hear the violent slamming of the front door as her husband went out of the house again. She had forgotten him.

Chapter Eleven

CHRISTOPHER had found no letters from Charlie among the papers. They were mostly letters from the children, and one or two from him. There was the first letter that Derek had ever written to her, beginning, "dere mumy", each letter about an inch high, and there was a painting of a very red cow in a very green field that Joy had done for her in her first term at school. There was an old diary that he opened with trembling fingers and a dragging sense of guilt. It consisted of notes of her social engagements, with occasionally some reference to the children ("Frank in bed with bad cold." "Went to school entertainment, Joy Red Riding Hood." "Derek's birthday party"). There were a few references to him ("Christopher gone to London to Medical Conference." "Christopher called up at 2 A.M. for Mrs. Handley's baby"). There was no mention of Charlie, though that was the year during which they had been seeing Charlie constantly. The lack of any mention of his name might mean nothing, of course, or it might mean everything. Susan was not the woman to pour out her heart on paper.

He wished that he had left the packet alone. The reading of the children's letters and the little diary had brought back memories of Susan as a young wife and mother—memories so vivid as to be almost unbearable.

He returned to his earlier resolution to forget. He must remember Susan, of course, but forget the words that she had said as she was dying. If he could not forget them, he must look on them as delirium, or as referring to something quite trivial. He had tried to do that before, but he had not been successful. Well, he must *make* himself do it. He seemed to be two people, the doctor and the patient. As the doctor, he took himself in hand with his old professional cunning.

"But, my dear fellow, it's as clear as daylight. If you weren't so run down, you'd see it in a moment. It's an insult to your wife to read that meaning into the words. Over and over again I've known the thoughts of dying people turn to some quite trivial event that has happened years ago. The fellow was always playing practical jokes on you. Well, he and your wife had obviously played one that you'd never tumbled to, and after all these years her clouded mind went back to it for no reason at all. There's no other possible explanation. You must pull yourself together."

And to himself, still the doctor, he said, "Poor devil! It's obvious enough what she meant."

The part of him that was the patient was docile, rather frightened, eager to help.

"Yes, I'm quite sure you're right. I'll do my best."

And he did his best. He settled down determinedly to his old routine. When he retired he had bought Frazer's *Golden Bough*, meaning to read it through, but his reading had been spasmodic, and he had only reached the middle of the second volume.

He planned out his time carefully. He would go to his study every morning, directly after breakfast, and sit down at his desk to read *The Golden Bough*. That, and the newspaper, would occupy his morning; in the afternoon he would go for a walk. Perhaps he would take up golf. The evening, of course, would be all right. There were books again, papers, the wireless, and people often asked him out to bridge. Looking back, he wondered vaguely how he had filled his time when Susan was alive. It had seemed to fill itself. She had been there, happy, eager, full of little plans. She was always calling him out to the garden to see some plant or bulb that was coming up. Susan could never realise that it was natural that something you planted in the autumn should come up in the spring. It always seemed a miracle to her.

"Darling, do come now, now. . . . I want to show you something. *Look!*"

"But you planted it, didn't you?"

"Yes, but isn't it wonderful?"

She was always wanting him to accompany her on her shopping expeditions, to help her choose things. They were both fond of music, and sometimes went to concerts in the evening. Generally, however, they spent the evening at home—he, reading desultorily, and she, sitting opposite him on the other side of the fireplace, sewing and retailing little pieces of gossip. The days had slipped by, as if a spell had been laid on them. He had hardly begun to do the things that he had always intended to do when he retired. He ought to have finished *The Golden Bough* by now, and begun Gibbon's *Decline and Fall*. . . . Well, he would set to work at once. He would put the thought and memory of Susan right out of his mind. He would draw up a time-table that would leave him no time to think. He would take up golf. Walking was a better exercise, but it gave one too much time to think.

His next door neighbours—the Wildens on one side, and the Sandersteads on the other—had been kind to him. The Wildens had asked him in to dinner the week after his return. They belonged to the class of the consciously and determinedly highbrow. Mrs. Wilden entertained him by a long discourse on the analogy of certain parts of Ibsen to certain parts of Shaw. He came home feeling depressed and exhausted. With Susan the Wildens had been amusing. When Mrs. Wilden reached sublimities of highbrowism, Susan, her blue eyes twinkling, would begin to praise Ethel M. Dell or Edgar Wallace, and bring the whole edifice crashing to the ground. Now that Susan was not there, the Wildens were amusing no longer.

It was the same with the Sandersteads. Mrs. Sanderstead altered the arrangement of every room in her house every week. You never found the sofa twice in the same place, and the bureau used to waltz round the room till, as Susan said, it made her feel dizzy. Not content with altering the furniture every week, Mrs. Sanderstead, who was a lady of considerable means, would occasionally make a clean sweep of everything—furniture, curtains, decorations—and start quite fresh with an entirely new period. Susan used to say that it gave her rather a shock to find Mrs.

Sanderstead still with the same husband throughout all these transformations. You felt that it was an oversight, and that he ought to have gone with the last *décor*, and been replaced by a new one. He was a small, silent man, with a permanently bewildered expression.

Christopher went to tea with them, and found the drawing-room passing through an oriental phase. Mrs. Sanderstead wore a mandarin's robe, and Mr. Sanderstead, as if in a pathetic attempt to accommodate himself to his new background, a large jade tie-pin.

Christopher spent a dreary afternoon with them, and decided to have a previous engagement the next time they invited him. Like the Wildens, the Sandersteads had suddenly and surprisingly ceased to be amusing, now that Susan was not there to laugh at them with him.

Lydia was looking after him with a sort of grim intensity. She regarded his well-being as a trust from Susan, and outraged her passion for economy by provisioning for him on a lavish scale. She made her housekeeping allowance, however, last a surprisingly long time, and Christopher suspected that she was stinting herself in order to make it go further. It gave Lydia acute pleasure to eat a meal that cost only a few pence.

When his study door was not shut properly, he could sometimes overhear Lydia's conversation with the milkman in the mornings. She cherished a brooding terror of Bolshevists, and believed that the country was riddled with plots to overthrow the Government and establish a Soviet. She had read a good deal of melodramatic fiction, and she knew that the less anyone looked like a spy, the more likely he was to be one. The milkman had aroused her terror, and amused himself by playing on it. He had convinced her that half the cabinet was in the pay of the Bolshevists, and that the Vicar of St. Mark's, an elderly man with a beard, was a Bolshevist agent.

"Well, it's only a question of months now," the milkman would say, and Lydia would answer with a "Go on," that was horrified, credulous, and greedy for more.

"Well, you'd be surprised if you knew some of the things I've heard the last day or two."

"It'd take something to surprise me."

"They're getting their men into the banks now as bank clerks. Then, when the time comes, they'll seize the banks and take all the money. It's all arranged down to the last detail. The Germans before the war were children to what they are."

"Get on with you," said Lydia, but the milkman knew that in her heart she believed him. She was already considering taking her savings out of the bank, and hiding them somewhere where they would be more easily accessible. The milkman had promised to let her know a day or two before the revolution broke out, because he had a cousin who knew a man who was in touch with the Reds.

Lydia thrilled to the stories. The excitement and terror they brought her seemed to fill some vital need of her being. In the old days Susan had often left the study door open on purpose, so that they could hear the conversation in the kitchen, but now he closed it with irritation whenever he heard Lydia's voice. He felt furious one day when he found a hoard of empty bottles and tins hidden in the tool shed, though he knew that if Susan had been there it would have been funny. Even Lydia had ceased to be entertaining now that Susan was not there to laugh at her with him.

He sat every morning in the study reading *The Golden Bough*. After some minutes he would find that he was reading the words without attention, and that his thoughts were again searching blindly in the past. ... Charlie had often met her when she went up to town for the day. She had been quite open about it. "I'll ask Charlie to meet me for lunch." Charlie used to come over, for the children's birthday parties. He always stayed the night on those occasions.

He brought his thoughts back with an effort to *The Golden Bough*, only to find a minute later that they were again with Charlie and Susan, riding into the country in that first mad car of Charlie's, wearing goggles, "scorching" horribly at thirty miles an hour. They had lunch at an inn, and Susan and Charlie went for a walk, while he fished in the river. He caught a trout, and Susan made him a laurel wreath.

He dragged his mind back again. It would get better in time. If, whenever he realised that his thoughts were wandering, he dragged them back, he would soon get them under control. But he didn't. They mutinied against him, they slipped the leash continually. He arranged with a professional to give him lessons in golf, but he took no interest in the game, and the professional became almost as bored as he was. He gave it up at the end of a week. The "children" were kind to him. They asked him to tea, and talked to him brightly, consolingly, but somehow they were not real to him. Only Susan and Charlie were real. Of the others Olivia was the most real. . . . Olivia, he felt, would have understood. . . .

He had not entered the drawing-room since the night he came home, but it began to have a strange, repellent attraction for him. He longed to open the door and go into it, but he dare not, because he knew that he would find Susan and Charlie there. . . .

Then he took himself in hand once more and faced the situation. He could not forget, he could not deceive himself. He must *know*. There must be someone who could tell him. An affair like that could not go on without someone's knowing about it. And suddenly he remembered Charlie's sisters, the three, rather prim spinsters (one had married, he remembered), who had brought Charlie up. He had not seen them since he and Charlie were boys together at Bart.'s, before he met Susan, but—they might know. Though Charlie had broken free from their control as soon as he could, they always seemed to hear of his peccadilloes. He was frequently being summoned to the old house in Somerset to be gently reprimanded, and given enough money to get himself out of the scrape. All Charlie's papers must have been sent to them. There must be letters of Susan's among them.

He sat down and wrote to Charlie's eldest sister, telling her that he would be motoring in Somerset next week, and asking if he might call and see them.

Chapter Twelve

CHRISTOPHER drove slowly down High Street, his suitcase on the back seat of the car. He was going to see Charlie's sisters. He had received a letter from the second one saying that they remembered him perfectly, and would be very glad to see him again. She added that they hoped he would stay the night.

The "children" had been very much interested in the expedition. Their eagerness showed him that they had felt uneasily responsible for him in his new loneliness, and that his having found an occupation, as they thought, was a great relief to them.

"It's a splendid idea, Father," Joy had said to him. "It'll give you a fresh interest, and take your mind right off things. And when you've done this tour in Somerset, and had a little rest, you must think out another tour—Scotland," vaguely, "or Cornwall, or Wales. It will be a continual interest. Bruce's cousin has retired, you know, and he takes a little motor tour every month or so. It's an excellent idea to look up as many old friends as possible by the way, too. It breaks the monotony, and it's better than putting up at hotels."

She spoke in the brisk, bright tones that she used to coax her children out of their little un-happinesses. ("Never mind, darling. Mummy's so sorry. Don't think about it. Look, play with this nice, new car. ...")

He was glad that they had taken it as a matter of course that he should suddenly want to go to Somerset. He had always hated the conventional "motor tour", but they had forgotten that. ...

He saw Jonathan suddenly among the crowds in High Street, ambling along, his hands in his pockets, whistling. He looked very long and thin and weedy and unkempt. His hair was unbrushed, his face and collar were dirty, his garterless stockings hung down over his shoes. Rachel's children were generally at one extreme or the other. Either she exhausted them and herself and the whole house by the energy and thoroughness with which she brushed and washed and cleaned them, or she let them go out without making any toilet at all.

Jonathan met Christopher's eye, and grinned blithely. Christopher pulled up, and Jonathan leapt upon the running board. He had obviously been bored, and welcomed a diversion.

"Well, what are you doing?" said Christopher.

"I'd be spending my Saturday twopence if I'd got it," said Jonathan, "but Mummy won't give it me because Barbara told tales."

Christopher forebore to enquire into this cryptic statement.

"Where's Barbara?"

"She can't come out. Brenda's got consumption," said Jonathan.

Christopher, of course, knew Brenda well. He had attended her for cancer, meningitis, tuberculosis, erysipelas, and an enlarged aorta. Jonathan was still hanging over the side of the car, evidently loth to be dismissed. There was something rather pathetic in his dirtiness and boredom. Christopher opened the door.

"Jump in," he said, "and I'll take you to the end of High Street."

Jonathan leapt into the seat beside Christopher. There he stretched out his long, slender body and said:

"Daddy's always too busy to take me in his," and added, "When I'm a man I'm going to have a motor 'bus instead of an ordinary car. I should think they're more fun to drive. There's no reason why an ordinary person shouldn't have one, is there?"

Christopher, on reflection, didn't think there was, and after that the conversation languished.

"What are you going to do this afternoon?" said Christopher at last.

Boredom settled down upon Jonathan again.

"Dunno," he said.

"Why don't you go to play with your cousins?"

"Auntie Joy hasn't asked me, and Mummy won't let me go when

she hasn't asked me. And besides," he added, "they'll probably only be going a walk with Miss Nash." He enunciated Miss Nash's name with deep contempt. "Playing silly games, and having silly fairy stories told them."

He put his hands in his pockets, and again stretched out his thin childish form in an attempt at a manly swagger.

"I say," he said, suddenly, "Gran used to give us all threepence every Saturday."

A crushing sense of remissness descended upon Christopher. He put his hand in his pocket and took out a two-shilling piece.

"Give half to Barbara," he said. "It's to make up for the other weeks. I'll give the others theirs when I come back. You must remind me about the threepence on Saturdays."

"Thanks awfully," said Jonathan, sitting up with a jerk, as he pocketed the coin. There was a sudden alertness in his wiry frame. His eyes had brightened in his sharp, grimy, little face. A penniless afternoon had been suddenly transformed to an afternoon that contained all the boundless possibilities that wealth can bestow upon it. But, as if aware of the sense of guilt that had come upon Christopher, and determined to pursue his advantage, he went on, "Aren't you ever going to have us to tea? Gran had us to tea every Saturday."

Christopher remembered. . . . Saturday had been a sort of gala-day to Susan. The "babies" in the afternoon, and the "children" in the evening. He could see her busily engaged upon her preparations for it, devising fresh treats, fresh surprises . . . jellies, blancmange, concoctions of fruit and cream in little glasses, animal biscuits, a cake in the shape of a little house, with chimney and windows and door. Joy, who made a fetish of nursery routine, used to be rather disapproving. "But, Mother dear, you needn't make such a *party* of it. Surely, just bread, and butter, and jam, and a sponge cake would be much better for them." After tea there were games, with little prizes arranged so that each one of them won a prize of some sort.

"I'm sorry," said Christopher. "I'd forgotten."

"We'll come next Saturday," said Jonathan, firmly. "I'll tell the others."

They had reached the end of High Street now, and Christopher drew up by the kerb.

"I must drop you here, old chap," he said.

"I'll go fishing this afternoon," said Jonathan, as he swung himself over the door without opening it, describing a parabola before he landed on his feet on the pavement. "I'll buy a new net, a sixpenny one, and some sweets, and go up to Henton Ponds. I'll get Barbara to come with me. I expect Brenda will be well by this afternoon."

For all his assumption of swaggering manliness Jonathan took Brenda's diseases quite seriously.

"Goodbye," said Christopher, as he moved off.

"Goodbye," called Jonathan; then with a vague impulse of politeness he added, "I hope you have a nice time."

Christopher reached the old-fashioned house in Somerset shortly before four. He thought that he had forgotten what it was like, but he remembered it again as soon as he saw it. It was a square red brick house, with a deep bay window on either side of the door; five windows in an orderly row showed the first floor, and above them were five other smaller windows. A semi-circular drive enclosed a piece of neatly mown grass, in the middle of which was a large, squat, holly bush. Venetian blinds and Nottingham lace curtains hung at all the windows. Nothing about it had changed. It had looked just like that on the day he and Charlie had driven up in the station cab to spend a weekend there. He had a sudden vivid memory of Charlie—handsome, merry, full of eager, pulsing life, leaning back in his seat and laughing uproariously over some joke as the cab turned in at the gate. He got out of the car and went slowly up the steps to the front door. His heart knocked against his ribs as he faced, for the first time, the monstrous nature of the errand on which he had come. He was going to ask these three inoffensive old ladies if they knew whether their dead brother had committed adultery with his dead wife nearly twenty years ago. Even though he realised the monstrousness of the task, he did not shrink from it. He was determined to go through with it now.

An elderly, housemaid opened the door, and Christopher stepped into the house. He found that he remembered that, too, quite well. Drawing-room on the left, dining-room on the right, the little morning-room behind the drawing-room. In the hall was a large glass case containing stuffed birds perched upon the branches of a tree, a Turkey carpet, and an enormous mahogany hatstand with innumerable pegs, flanked by two Cromwell chairs.

The housemaid showed him into the drawing-room. A cabinet, with glass doors, filled with a curious mixture of real treasures and rubbishy souvenirs from foreign places, stood in the corner opposite the door, next to a walnut whatnot. In the middle of the room was a *tête-à-tête* seat in faded damask. An elaborately tiered fern stand stood in the window between the Nottingham lace curtains. On the marble mantelpiece was an ormolu clock, and on either side of it wax flowers under glass cases. There was a white fur rug at the hearth, and before the fireplace a screen made of papier mâché, inlaid with mother-of-pearl. A piano against the wall was covered with old-fashioned photographs in silver frames, and near it was a little work-table, with a neat pile of leather-bound books upon a fringed mat.

It was all uncompromisingly Victorian, but the room was so high and well proportioned, the surface of the furniture shone so warmly with the unremitting polishings of years, that the general effect was pleasing. It had, however, the elusive, but unmistakable, atmosphere of a room that is only used upon formal occasions.

The door opened suddenly, and Charlie's youngest sister came in. She did not seem to Christopher much older than she had seemed on his former visit. Or, rather, she had seemed preternaturally old then, and he found her now younger than he had expected. Her hair, flecked with grey, was still dressed as he remembered it dressed in the old days, drawn up into a bun on the top of her head, leaving a cascade of unattached hairs to fall down at the back. She wore a jumper, rather like a dressing-jacket in shape, over a full, long serge skirt. Her expression was kind and cheerful, and her shortsightedness gave her a questing look, as if she were searching for something.

Christopher remembered her brief, ill-fated romance. She had married, when she was thirty, a man who spent all her money, and drank himself to death in two years. She had returned to her sisters penniless.

She greeted Christopher with a nervous excitement that showed him, for the first time, what a tremendous event his visit was in the lives of the sisters.

"So kind of you to come," she fluttered. "Will you come into the morning-room? I think it's more comfortable than this room. Miss Brooks is there. She's my sister's companion. Sarah's companion, you know. You're such an old friend that we needn't stand on ceremony, need we?"

She led him out into the hall and to the morning-room. It was evident that she was a little doubtful of the propriety of the proceeding.

"After all, we're very old friends," she repeated, as she opened the door, "and we're all so fond of this little room."

The little room proclaimed itself as a room that was loved and lived in. It was cluttered up with books, writing materials, sewing, magazines. It contained shabby easy chairs and a shabby sofa. There was a round table in the middle of the room, covered with a chenille cloth, on which was a bowl of roses. A sewing machine stood in the window, and against the wall was a "davenport" and an enormous bookcase with glass doors, behind which he saw bound volumes of *Household Words, Leisure Hour,* and *Sunday at Home.* On a fretwork bracket, near the door, was a faded photograph of three pretty girls, wearing bustles and flounces and tiny hats. A Pomeranian slept in a basket by the fire. The room had a warm, cosy, intimate atmosphere. It was full of the mysterious currents of human relationships.

"This is Miss Brooks," said Agatha.

Miss Brooks was about Agatha's age. Her face wore the same kind, eager, rather child-like expression. She did her hair in the same way, with the same cascade of hair escaping from the back of the bun. Her jumper was of the same shape, though made of different material. Miss Brooks had probably made both jumpers at the sewing machine that stood between the windows. Christopher remembered again that Agatha had no money of her own. Her position in the house would be very different from that of her sisters. He sensed a half-furtive friendship between the two women. Miss Brooks greeted him with an effusive cordiality that had nothing insincere in it.

"A visitor is such an event to us," she said. "We live so very quietly. I don't think that any of us have slept a wink since we knew that you were coming."

He made some conventional response, his thoughts far away. Charlie and Susan . . . things like that did not happen in this little Victorian world, shut away behind its Venetian blinds and Nottingham lace curtains. One passed by references to it in newspapers without reading them, one returned to the library, unread, books in which they found a place. ("I simply can't think why people write about that sort of thing. I want a nice book about nice people, with a happy ending, please.")

"Except poor Adelaide," Agatha said with a sigh.

"Does Mr. Mainwaring know about poor Miss Adelaide?" said Miss Brooks.

"I don't think so," said Agatha, and, as she turned to him, the eager brightness of her smile clouded over. "She's———." She paused for a word, and went on, without having found it. "She doesn't know any of us now."

"It's senile decay," whispered Miss Brooks.

"We told her about your visit, of course, but I don't suppose she really took it in."

"Of course, she's better on some days than on others," said Miss Brooks.

"I hope Sarah won't be cross with me for bringing Mr. Mainwaring in here," said Agatha. "She thinks me so very unconventional."

The two women smiled at each other, and again he was aware of something innocently conspiratorial in their friendship.

It was obvious, too, that Agatha derived a certain amount of pleasure from being the youngest of the three. Christopher, watching her eager excitement over his visit, her rather pleased consciousness of her daring in entertaining him in the morning-room instead of the drawing-room, found it almost impossible to believe that she had left this sheltered world for two years, during which her scoundrel of a husband had bled her dry. He wondered if she had suffered very much, if she had hated her husband, and resented her lot, or if she had accepted it with this eager childlikeness, seeing the scoundrel as a hero, gladly giving him her little all. It had certainly left no abiding mark upon her.

Then the Pomeranian woke up, and had to be introduced to Christopher. His name was Prince, and he was an important member of the family circle. He looked elderly, and dyspeptic, and bad-tempered, but the part he played in their lives was that of beloved, wayward child.

"He's such a naughty boy when he goes out shopping with us," said Agatha. "Miss Clare, at the little confectioner's, always gives him a chocolate drop, and he simply won't pass the shop now without having his chocolate. He makes us go in whether we've anything to buy there or not." As they talked, the picture of the life they led grew clearer. Every minute of every day mapped out. Every day, to the smallest detail, like the day that had gone before. The only excitements, the entertainment (at tea only) of a small, select elderly circle, whose lives and interests were the same as theirs. There was about them that placid serenity, childlike and complacent, that marks women who lead sheltered, ordered lives. Slight disturbing events there were in the family circle, but nothing that affected it deeply.

They had come even to take Adelaide's senile decay for granted. Sarah was easily upset, rather jealous of Agatha's friendship with Miss Brooks, but the love they bore each other was the deep unalterable love of people who have no ties outside the world they have made for themselves. Their house and garden, the little village happenings, bounded their vision on all sides. The trial of a new cake recipe the planting of a new flower, was a week's event. If Prince sneezed, their world was shaken to its foundations.

Both Agatha and Sarah had weak eyesight, and could not read for long. Every evening Miss Brooks read aloud to them, and, when the story grew too exciting, Sarah's nerves "went to pieces" suddenly, and she ordered Miss Brooks to stop. That had happened last night.

"We'd just got to the most thrilling part," said Agatha. "When Sarah said: 'I can't bear any more; shut the book up.' Then she went to bed, and Miss Brooks had to take the book with them—you see Miss Brooks sleeps in Sarah's room on account of her rheumatism—because, of course, when Sarah gets upset over a book like that, she sometimes finds that, although she can't bear to hear any more just then, still she can't go to sleep till she knows what happened. So Miss Brooks has to finish it to herself, and then tell Sarah, very quietly, what happens."

"She didn't last night," said Miss Brooks. "She couldn't sleep, and yet she wouldn't let me tell her what happened. I skimmed through the book before we got into bed, so as to have it ready. Of course, I think it was the thought of your visit that had over-excited her. We had a very restless night."

"I had, too," eagerly confided Agatha. "It was your visit, partly, of course, but, partly, it was leaving the story at such a thrilling point. I felt as if I couldn't live without knowing whether they made it up. You see, the hero and heroine had quarrelled, and there was a dreadful man who wanted to marry the heroine, and had even had a notice of her engagement to him put into the newspapers without her knowledge, and sent it to the hero, who was abroad. Well, you can imagine what it felt like to have to stop there. But Miss Brooks was very kind. She managed to scribble on a piece of paper how it ended, and pushed it under my door when she went to turn out the bathroom light."

"Wasn't it naughty of me?" said Miss Brooks, and they laughed together, like a couple of schoolgirls who have outwitted a mistress.

"Miss Sarah had such a bad night that we thought it best for her to stay in bed till tea-time to-day," went on Miss Brooks, "especially as it was to be such a *very* exciting day." She glanced at her watch. "It's time I went to help her dress."

"My sister's right hand is crippled with rheumatism," said Agatha, "so she needs Miss Brooks's help a good deal."

Miss Brooks glanced at the table, and her eye fell upon a piece of paper, on which a crossword puzzle had been drawn and filled in.

"Oh dear," she said, as she tore it up and put it into the waste-paper basket, "we mustn't leave that lying about."

"Sarah hates to see us doing crossword puzzles together," explained Agatha, "because they don't interest her at all. So we daren't do them in the real newspaper. We copy them out, and do them when she isn't there."

And again they laughed, like a couple of naughty children.

Then Miss Brooks went out, and he was left alone with Agatha, and at once the reality of the little enclosed world vanished, and Charlie and Susan became real again. He had come to ask these women if they knew anything, or had known anything, and he must ask them. He must drag it out of them somehow. They might have known and forgotten. They might even be able to tell him something that meant nothing to them, but would make everything clear to him.

He must go slowly, of course. He mustn't frighten them. Agatha was telling him about Miss Brooks. Miss Brooks had originally been companion to a cousin of theirs, and had come to them for a short holiday after the cousin's death. They had found her so invaluable that she had stayed on with them, officially as Susan's companion. Christopher waited until she had finished telling him this, and then gradually brought the conversation to Charlie, reminding her of the week-end that he had spent there years ago with Charlie. After that it was easy to discuss Charlie. What a pity it was that he had not married and had children. He was so fond of children. But, perhaps, he had had some disappointment. Perhaps the woman he loved would not, or could not, marry him. He introduced Susan's name casually, watching Agatha closely. She was vague and rather bewildered. It was plain that she had forgotten the mischievous young spark who had been Charlie, and remembered only a non-existent saint, winged and haloed.

"Poor dear Charlie," she said vaguely, "such a good boy."

Then Sarah and Miss Brooks came in. Sarah was stout and dignified, and opulently dressed in a full old-fashioned dress of purple silk, with a good deal of jewelry. She must have been much handsomer than Agatha when they were young. There was something imperious in her air and movements. It was clear that she was the ruling spirit in the household. She treated Christopher with a distant graciousness that was very different from Agatha's fluttering excitement.

"Your visit is a very great pleasure to us, Mr. Mainwaring," she said, holding out her arm with a gesture that seemed to disown the crippled, twisted hand at the end of it.

The elderly housemaid was spreading a cloth over the round table in the middle of the room. Sarah's brow drew into a regal frown.

"I thought we'd decided to have tea in the drawing-room," she said.

Agatha fluttered nervously.

"Yes, dear, but somehow when Mr. Mainwaring came—he's *quite* an old friend, you know, and this room's so much more friendly."

Sarah heaved a sigh of resignation.

"She's so impulsive," she said to Christopher, and he saw that she still thought of Agatha as the headstrong girl who had insisted on marrying the scoundrel against everyone's advice.

During tea they talked to Christopher in a sort of trio, interrupting each other continually.

"We planted them in the autumn——"

"It was the spring we planted them, dear."

"And not a single one came up."

"Just one or two did, dear, but such miserable things."

"And Dr. Goodwood said——"

"I think it was the Vicar who told us, dear."

"Oh yes. Anyway he told us that it was putting ashes on them——"

"He said fresh ashes, dear. Of course it would have been all right if they'd been kept in the air for a few weeks first."

After tea Agatha suggested a game of whist.

"We generally play three-handed," she said. "It will be such a treat to play four. Poor Adelaide, of course, can't play now."

They played whist till the dressing-bell rang, then Christopher changed in a large bedroom overlooking the lawn. An enormous mahogany wardrobe took up the whole of one side of it. Over the bed was a text—God is Love—the letters carved in fretwork against a green plush background. The bedstead was of brass, ornamented with innumerable knobs and circles. There was a thick white fringed counterpane on the bed. Dinner was served in the large Victorian dining-room by the elderly maid. He could not possibly question them now, of course. Later, in the intimacy of the long evening, he would bring the subject round to Charlie again. But after dinner Adelaide came down. She did not come down every evening, apparently, but this evening she had sensed some unusual excitement in the atmosphere of the house, and had decided to investigate. Her advent was heralded by her attendant—a pretty, faded-looking woman in a nurse's uniform. ("We daren't leave her alone a minute now," said Agatha.) It was a very regal figure that appeared in the wake of the nurse: taller, handsomer, more dignified even than Sarah. She was dressed in a gown of grey moiré silk, with lace collar and cuffs. She sailed into the room, her head held high, and spoke in a loud aside to her attendant.

"Who are these people, dear? You must introduce me."

The attendant introduced her. She greeted her sisters and Christopher with elaborate courtesy. ("She never knows them," whispered Miss Brooks to Christopher, "she always has to be introduced.") Then she sat and talked to the company politely about the events of her girlhood, only it was clear that to her they were not the events of her girlhood, they were contemporary events.

At half-past nine she looked at the clock uneasily, and said: "Papa was to have called for me at nine. I can't think why he's so late."

She grew more and more distressed as the evening wore on.

"I can't think what's happened to Papa," she said. "I'm so ashamed to be inflicting myself on you like this. It's unpardonable."

Her agitation became rather painful. She asked if they had a manservant who could see her home. Perhaps there had been a misunderstanding. .... They would be so worried about her at home.

"I don't know what you'll think of me, staying like this," she said. "Papa must have been detained somewhere."

Sarah asked her to stay the night. She refused.

"Of *course* not. .... It's so kind of you, but I couldn't dream of such a thing. Papa will be here any minute, he must have been detained. I hope he hasn't had an accident."

Worn out at last by anxiety, she allowed herself to be led away to bed, apologising profusely for the trouble she was giving, still deeply agitated about what could have happened to Papa.

Christopher had found the scene distressing, but the sisters took it as a matter of course.

"That always happens when she comes downstairs," said Sarah, "she's really happier upstairs, and she's very fond of her nurse. They cut out paper patterns together, though you have to watch her with the scissors."

Christopher glanced at the old-fashioned photograph of three pretty, smiling girls, wearing bustles, and flounced dresses, and tiny hats. He felt a vague pity that was partly fear. .... It was impossible to talk of Susan after that.

"We've given you Charlie's room," said Sarah, as they said good night.

He woke in the night in a sudden sweat of anger and jealousy. Charlie's face seemed to be mocking him through the darkness. Charlie's lazy laughing voice seemed to be saying, "Don't you wish you knew!"

He cursed the weakness and timidity that had held him bound. "I won't leave this house," he boasted to himself in the darkness, "till it's told me all it knows. I'll ask them outright to-morrow morning if there were any letters from Susan." Yet, even as he said it, something deep down in him knew that he would not ask them.

Only Agatha and Miss Brooks appeared at breakfast. Sarah had been over-excited by his visit, and had not slept. Quite suddenly Agatha began to talk about Charlie.

"It was very, very painful," she said. "Of course, they sent all his private papers here—letters and notes, and diaries, and things like that. We burnt them all unread. We felt that we'd no right to read anything like that, even though he was dead."

It was as if the question in his mind were so insistent that she had had to answer it, without knowing why.

They fluttered about him while he had breakfast, and made up a little packet of sandwiches, cakes, and apples for his lunch. ("I think it's so much better when you're motoring. You can't trust these chance inns, I'm sure.")

Agatha went into the garden to get him some roses to take home with him.

"I'm afraid the frost will soon get them now. It's nice of you to have come to see us. It's been such an event. We shall talk of it for years!"

He drove away with the little packet of sandwiches and the bunch of roses on the seat beside him.

Chapter Thirteen

"WHAT are we going to do?" said Olivia.

She looked away as she spoke, as if she dare not meet Stephen's eyes.

It was their first meeting since the one that had been interrupted by the sound of Derek's key in the lock. Stephen had rung her up, and asked her to meet him at the Henton 'bus terminus. She had known why he had suggested that. What they had to discuss could not be discussed in Derek's house or in his.

He had been waiting for her when she got down from the 'bus, and they had walked quickly, without speaking, along the road that ran across the highest point of the common, past the war memorial on one side, and the old windmill on the other. From the road a riot of golden bracken, silver birches, and beeches gilded by the first touch of frost, spread down the hill-side to a pond that gleamed blue and motionless through the branches.

There was a sharp tang in the air, a faint luminous mist over the horizon. They came to the main road that joined the road from the common, crossed it, and climbed a stile that led to a public pathway through a private estate. On Sunday afternoon this pathway was a favourite haunt of courting couples, family parties, and children. To-day it was empty but for Olivia and Stephen. It wound in and out of the trees till it reached a massive oak tree that blocked the way, making it swerve sharply to either side. The tree was enormous, prehistoric, iron girt. A seat ran round it, and on to the trunk of the tree was affixed a notice, announcing that here two famous statesmen had once sat to discuss England's policy at a crucial moment of her affairs.

They sat down on the seat, just below the notice, and Olivia spoke for the first time.

"What are we going to do?"

Stephen looked at her. He was pale, and the furrows on his cheeks showed deeply.

"There isn't any question of what we're going to do," he said, shortly. "You must come away with me."

Olivia still stared fixedly into the distance. Her breast was rising and falling quickly.

"What about Wanda?" she said.

"Wanda and I are nothing to each other. We haven't lived together for years."

"You haven't told her?"

"No. . . . The only question is, of course, whether she'll divorce me."

She turned and looked at him.

"Does that make any difference?"

"It makes a little." He laid his hand over hers on the seat. "Things won't be too pleasant at first, but once the break's made, it's made for ever."

The forced calm left his voice. "Olivia . . . tell me you'll come with me."

She took her hand away from his, and pressed it against the other in her lap.

"I don't know what to say, Stephen. Ever since I've known, I've gone over and over things in my mind till I feel insane. I've not slept. I've hardly known what I'm doing. Going away seems so—impossible somehow."

He was silent for a long time, then said evenly.

"We needn't go away, of course."

"Oh, no, I couldn't bear *that*."

"Then we must go away."

"Yes."

"Would Derek divorce you?"

"I think so." She smiled bitterly. "Derek always likes to do the correct thing."

Again there was silence. Then he said gently:

"Do you think you'll regret it? Is there any doubt in your mind?"

She drew in her breath sharply.

"How can you ask me that, Stephen?"

"That's settled then. We'll go away."

He spoke quietly, soothingly, as if she had been a distraught child. Her emotion touched him the more because he knew her to be deeply reserved, knew that she held her emotions generally under iron control.

She sat gazing in front of her, looking very slender and childlike in her severe navy coat and skirt. He loved her so much that, for a second, he found it in his heart to wish that she need not have had to go through this, almost found it in his heart to wish, for her sake, that she had not loved him.

"It will ruin you professionally," she said slowly. "What are you going to do? I have only thirty pounds a year."

"I can start at the beginning and work my way up. We can go somewhere where no one knows us, and start fresh."

She looked at him with a rather crooked smile.

"There isn't such a place. Everyone will know about it before we have been there a year. You know that a tale like that never dies. You remember the Mortons. . . ."

He remembered the Mortons—a young doctor and his wife, who had come to Ravenham, and who had quickly attained a good social and professional position in the town. After two years, it was discovered that they were not married, because the woman's husband had refused to divorce her, and a year later they left the town without a penny.

He chaffed her gently.

"Darling, this isn't like you. Are you afraid to take the risk?"

"Oh, it isn't that," she said with sudden passion. "You know it isn't that. It's—we must think of *everything*. We mustn't do this thing rashly, and regret it afterwards. People are broad-minded, I know, but a professional man's position is—different. I shall have ruined your career. It's a heavy responsibility for me to take."

"Dear, you're making it all too complicated. I love you, and you love me. That's simple, isn't it? And that's all there is to it. We may not be able to live in luxury, but I shan't let you starve. You may be sure of that."

"I wasn't thinking of myself."

"I know, but you needn't think of me either. I've got my brain and my hands. I can make good, even if I have to give up my profession."

She glanced at his face—sensitive, dreamy, the face of an artist. He was more at home in his study, among his first editions, and antiques, and prints, than in his office. He was conscientious and hardworking, but it was his father who had made the position into which he had stepped. She could not imagine him entering the rough-and-tumble competition of life. She had a sudden searing vision of him: bewildered, shabby, a failure, drifting from one unsuitable job to another. It was not as if he were a young man. His hair was grizzled at the temples, his tall figure stooped. . . . Could her love, could any woman's love, make up for it?

"And I don't suppose I shall have to do that," he went on. "If Wanda divorces me, everything will be plain sailing."

"You said something like that before. Do you think that Wanda won't divorce you?"

"One's never sure of Wanda's doing anything. . . . I'll ask her. She may as well know now, as later, how things are."

"What exactly will you tell her?"

"I won't mention your name, of course. I'll simply tell her that I've decided to leave her."

"She'll want alimony."

"She'll want everything she can get."

She was silent. He put his hand again protectively over hers, and smiled at her.

"Darling, you don't know—you'll never know—how much I love you."

A sudden exaltation of happiness seized her, then died away, leaving her spirit cold and dead.

"I think I'm tired," she said unsteadily. "I can't believe it. It's like telling each other a fairy tale."

He raised her hand and pressed it to his lips.

"You're going through the worst time now. Once you've gone away, everything will be different. You've nothing to worry yourself with, dearest. It won't hurt Derek, you know. He's encased in selfishness."

"No, it won't hurt Derek," she said dreamily. "It will hurt Derek's father more than Derek. I shall be sorry to do that."

"I think the old man will understand."

"He won't. When people have been happily married, they don't understand."

"He doesn't matter, anyway. Olivia . . . you love me?"

She turned her eyes to him, and spoke slowly in a low voice.

"I love you with all my heart."

"Our way's quite clear then. I'll speak to Wanda. If she'll divorce me, well and good. If not—still well and good. We'll go in any case."

"When?"

"As soon as we can. We needn't wait longer than it will take to pack. I can't wait. . . . I've loved you too long."

She said slowly, "Stephen, I can't——"

She stopped.

"Can't what?"

She went on as if with an effort. "I can't leave Derek just now. I want to leave him. I don't love him. I'd feel nothing but joy if somebody told me that I'd never see him again, but—he's frightened and unhappy. It's his business. He won't tell me anything, but I know that it's doing badly. I couldn't leave him just now. I'd feel like a rat leaving a sinking ship. Just let me wait a little longer. Just till things have come round."

"That's sentiment, dear."

"I don't know what it is. Only—I know I must. Things can't go on as they are much longer. I can tell that. If his affairs actually go smash, he'll be glad to be rid of me. If they recover, he won't mind my going, except for the humiliation, but just now when he's fighting, when he needs all his energy and thought for his business, I can't—run away. It might be just the last straw to him."

"What has he ever done for you that you should consider him?"

"Nothing. But—give me till the end of next month. Things will have turned one way or the other by then."

"And if they haven't?"

"Then I'll come with you."

They were silent. The wood was very still. Not a branch stirred. No bird was singing. There were no sounds from the road. They might have been in the heart of a forest. . . . On all sides stretched the red gold undergrowth, bracken and crimson bramble on a carpet of fallen beech leaves. Above them the trees still held part of their autumn glory. . . . The air was full of a strange sweet melancholy. It weighed upon Olivia's spirit, till it was almost more than she could bear. She tried to look forward, to see her life fulfilled at last with love, and she could feel nothing but this weary, aching hopelessness. The evening mist was closing in upon them through the trees. She shivered.

"You're cold," he said. "We must be going home."

She rose obediently. Suddenly his arms were about her, and she clung to him shaken by a sudden tempest of sobs.

"Don't, don't," he said. "What is it? . . . Tell me.

"I love you so," she sobbed. "I'm frightened."

He reassured her, and would have held her to him more tightly, but she broke loose, checking her sobs, and wiping the tears from her pale cheeks.

They began to walk back to the road over the dead moist leaves. The sun hung low in the sky like a red ball. He gave her his hand at the stile, and, as she took it, she had a sudden revealing flash of knowledge of him: his patience, his kindness, his utter goodness. They would have been so happy if they had met in time. Life seemed so wantonly, senselessly, cruel.

They walked, still in silence, over the common to the point where the 'bus started for Ravenham. Once Stephen said with unconvincing cheerfulness, "Well, we've thrashed everything out, haven't we?"

And she said, "Yes."

But both of them knew that they had not thrashed everything

out. They had not mentioned Clarissa, though she had been in the thoughts of both of them all the time.

Chapter Fourteen

JONATHAN walked up to the front door, and knocked very loudly nine times. He always knocked nine times because he was nine years old. Lydia answered the knock breathlessly.

"Whatever!" she exclaimed indignantly. "It's enough to deafen a body."

"I've come about the party," said Jonathan, entering and wiping his shoes on the mat with a business-like air. His stockings hung down over his shoes, and his exposed legs were adorned with innumerable ink drawings of skulls and cross-bones.

"What party?" said Lydia.

The milkman had just left her, and her mind was full of pictures of Chinese Bolshevists, engaged in manufacturing instruments of torture behind the blinds of their innocent-seeming laundries. "Chinks?" the milkman had said. "They're the finest torturers the world has ever known." It was difficult for her to bring her thoughts down to Jonathan and his affairs.

"This afternoon's party," said Jonathan impatiently. "Where's Grandad?"

"He's busy," said Lydia, barring his way, but Jonathan had already squirmed his thin person past her, and was opening the study door.

Christopher looked up with a start from *The Golden Bough*. He was reading it without interest, doggedly, determinedly, going back to re-read a paragraph whenever he found that his thoughts had wandered.

"Hello," he said. He was conscious of a sudden constraint that was almost shyness. When Susan was alive he had seldom seen his grandchildren except in her company, and his relations with them had been pleasant and easy. He had not realised then that it had been Susan who had made them so. The children had come and gone as they pleased. He talked to them if he felt inclined, and, if he felt disinclined, left them to Susan. He remembered that Jonathan, when he was a tiny boy, had asked what "queen" meant. When it had been explained to him he was silent for a few minutes, and then had said, "Gran's our queen, isn't she?"

"Hello," he said again, in a tone that asked Jonathan his errand.

"I've come to help," said Jonathan.

"Help?"

"Yes—the party. I used to come in the mornings and help Gran."

Christopher's feeling of dismay increased.

"What do you mean?"

Jonathan was obviously controlling his impatience with difficulty.

"The tea and the games. Have you thought of what games we're going to have?"

"Er—no."

"Or got prizes?"

"No."

"And what are we going to have for tea?"

"I don't know," said Christopher, feeling like a criminal before his judge, and added in a feeble attempt at self-defence, "I told Lydia you were coming to tea."

"Did you say jelly in little glasses, with cream on?"

"No."

"We always have those. And chocolate biscuits, and crackers. Have you looked to see if there are any crackers?"

"No. Where did—where are they kept?"

"Don't you know that?" said Jonathan sternly, "I'll show you."

In the dining-room he threw open the door of the sideboard cupboard, and burrowed in it like a small rabbit, leaving only his ink-adorned legs exposed to view. Then he emerged triumphantly with a highly-coloured box.

"*There!*" he said. "There *is* one. I thought there might be. She used to buy a lot at once." He handed it to Christopher. "It's a nice one, isn't it? She always used to get nice ones."

Christopher took the box and held it in silence. The memory of Susan had become unbearably vivid again. Susan, smiling and happy, bustling about the house on a Saturday morning, intent on her "baby party" preparations, laughing at Lydia's attempts to keep down the expenses of it, tying the prizes with coloured ribbons, decorating the table with a miniature Zoo, or an Old Woman that Lived in a Shoe, or a little farmyard.

Jonathan broke into his reverie abruptly.

"May I go and look at her picture?"

"Yes."

"Will you come too?"

"No."

Jonathan slipped into the big empty drawing-room, and Christopher went back into the study, where he stood by the window, his heart beating unevenly, gazing out over the garden.

Soon he heard the closing of the drawing-room door, and Jonathan joined him.

"She's in Heaven, isn't she?" said Jonathan, then, without waiting for an answer, went on, "I shan't go to Heaven when I die, because I tell stories."

"Why do you tell them?" said Christopher vaguely, feeling that some response was necessary.

"I tell them to Mummie. I say 'yes', when she asks if I've come straight home from school, and if I've wiped my boots, and I say I haven't got my feet wet when I have, and things like that. Because if I don't, she goes on, and on, and on, and on."

He threw a sly glance at Christopher. "Daddy tells her stories sometimes, too. I've heard him. He says that people he met asked how she was, and sent regards and things when they didn't, 'cause I was with him and heard. . . ." He stopped a minute, then went on resignedly, "But I'd go to Hell anyway, 'cause I do lots of other things besides that. I fight, and I'm greedy, and I like teasing Barbara, and I hate Sunday School and Scripture. I'm *sick* of the Israelites," he said with sudden vehemence, "and their plagues, and commandments, and things. . . . Do they let the people in Heaven come and see the people in Hell?"

"I believe not," said Christopher.

A smile of radiant sweetness broke out on Jonathan's small keen face.

"They won't stop Gran coming to see me," he said confidently. "She'll come and see me whatever they say. And she won't let them hurt me either. She's the only person in the whole world," he ended, suddenly disconsolate, "who's never been cross with me."

"Well, what about this party?" said Christopher.

"Let's go to Lydia, and tell her just what we want," said Jonathan, slipping his hand into Christopher's, and drawing him to the door. The hand in Christopher's was a baby's hand, soft, thin, confiding. The heavy weight of responsibility descended again upon Christopher's spirit.

Miss Nash arrived first, bringing Dickie, and Billy, and Laura. They were immaculately clean and neat. Miss Nash was rather breathless. She had been telling them a story to beguile the journey, and it had been a difficult task, as Billy demanded adventure stories, and Laura cared only for fairy stories, and Dickie thought it beneath his dignity to be told stories by Miss Nash at all.

Miss Nash was one of those people who imagine that children must be perpetually entertained. She had a series of "talking games" that they played on their walks, and an endless supply of stories with different characters, the threads of which she could take up at any moment. She looked very worn, and bright, and eager as she handed her charges over to Christopher. The clasp of her hand and the lowered tone of her voice expressed a sympathy that he felt ought not to have irritated him as much as it did.

Jonathan and Barbara arrived just as she was telling Christopher what Laura had said in bed last night. Jonathan and Barbara greeted her coldly. Barbara would have liked Miss Nash because of her wonderful powers of story-telling, but Jonathan despised her, so Barbara felt that she must despise her too.

Jonathan had been subjected to one of Rachel's tempestuous cleaning operations. Rachel, unduly sensitive to criticism from Joy, was determined that, when Joy saw him at Christopher's, she should have no fault to find with him. So she scrubbed him and brushed him, till, driven almost to madness, he rebelled. There was a scene, she mastered him in a physical struggle, he sobbed out insults at her, she replied by passionate reproaches. Finally, still rebellious, he set off with Barbara; and Rachel, whose head always ached badly after a tussle with Jonathan, went to lie down and indulge in one of her orgies of self-pity.

Jonathan's nerves were frayed by the scene, and when he set off he felt thoroughly angry and naughty. As Barbara was the only person present, he vented his mood upon her. He disobeyed her anxious instructions to keep himself tidy, he refused even to go the direct way to Christopher's, he dragged his shoes in the gutter, he climbed on to a wall, he got through a hedge into some one's garden, he swung on somebody's gate, he tried to climb some tall iron railings, deliberately dirtying his suit, face, and hands in the process. It was at this point that Barbara, unable to bear any more, burst into tears of shame and misery at his plight.

Her tears stirred him to a sense of vague compunction, and he walked with her, silent but decorous, till they reached Christopher's. Miss Nash noticed his dirty hands and face, his untidy hair and dusty suit, with unconscious satisfaction. The unkemptness of the little Main-warings (Barbara's face was streaked where she had wiped away her tears) emphasised the neatness and cleanliness of her own charges, and the contrast sent a warm glow to Miss Nash's heart.

Dickie was watching Jonathan with fascinated absorption. Jonathan had for Dickie the glittering allure of evil. He was the incarnation of attractive wickedness. He did all the forbidden things—he fought, he was impertinent and disobedient, he climbed trees, he was dirty and untidy, he raced about the streets with "common" boys. And withal he was swaggering and debonair and defiant. One part of Dickie adored him, and the other part was afraid of him. There was in Dickie a secret fear of life that had originated with the episode of the stolen toy monkey. Joy's words had gone deeper than she had thought or intended. Often he dreamt now that he had stolen things—ridiculous things like feathers or pokers, or even once a camel—and that policemen had come to take him to prison. He would wake up gasping and sobbing in a terror that would lie over his spirit all day.

When they went into the fields beyond Henton Common, he was frightened now even of picking wild flowers. He pretended that he did not want to pick them, but really he was frightened. There was a picture in one of his story books of a man in prison. He was lying on the floor of a room no bigger than a cupboard, with a tiny barred window high up in the wall. There was nothing for him to sit on, or to lie on, but the floor. He was dressed in rags, with iron chains on his feet; there was a jug of water and a piece of bread on the floor, and a large rat watched him from a corner of the room. Dickie hated rats.

"What have you done to yourself?" said Christopher suddenly to Jonathan.

Jonathan looked down at his wrist.

"Oh, I cut it last week."

"His penknife slipped," said Barbara.

His penknife had not slipped, though that was what he had told Rachel. It was his Person who had dared him to cut his wrist as hard as he could with his new penknife. His Person was always daring him to do things like that. Once it had dared him to put his finger in the candle flame and hold it there, and he had done it. Sometimes his Person dared him to climb from tree to tree, or to walk on walls at dizzy heights. He did not know what his Person looked like. He only heard it daring him to do things, and laughing at him when he did not do them. There was one dare he had not taken yet, and that was to put his foot under the wheel of a cart as it passed him in the street. His Person laughed every time he met one and did not do it, and he knew that he would have to do it in the end. He knew, too, that once he had put his foot under a cart wheel his Person would leave him alone.

They played the usual games after tea—Dumb Crambo, Blind Man's Buff, Hunt the Thimble.

As they played, a heavy depression began to weigh upon Jonathan's spirit. It wasn't a bit like one of Gran's parties. They were the same people, playing the same games, and yet all the fun had gone out of it. Grandad was doing things as if he wasn't really there, as if he didn't care what happened. When you spoke to him, he answered you as if he wasn't listening to himself, and didn't know what he was saying.

And Barbara was bossing. He hated Barbara when she bossed. She was ordering them all about, and telling them what to do, trying to be like Gran. And Grandad didn't care what any of them did. It was *horrible*. ... The others didn't seem to notice it. They were playing and laughing just as if it was all right, as if Gran was with them, as if Barbara wasn't bossing so hatefully, and Grandad only pretending to be there. A sudden sense of loneliness swept over Jonathan. It was a familiar enough sensation, and it came, strangely, most often when he was with a lot of people. It was a feeling of not belonging. No one knew about it except Jonathan himself. He was popular and had a host of boy followers. But it was when he was playing most keenly, when he seemed most part of the group around him that this terrifying sense of loneliness would suddenly descend upon him. He had never had it at these parties before, because always before Gran had been there, and no one could feel lonely with Gran. But this afternoon it came upon him, and grew stronger and stronger, till it was a sort of panic. He fought against it, becoming rough and noisy, shouting and upsetting the game, to prove to himself that he wasn't miles and miles away from them all. His anger with Barbara increased. Her shrill little voice ordering them about, pretending to be Gran, infuriated him.

"Shut up!" he shouted to her rudely, "you beastly old Jemima, shut up!"

It always made Barbara cry to be called Jemima. She began to cry now. Jonathan danced round her exultantly.

"Cry baby! Cry baby! Silly little cry baby!"

It was at this point that Joy arrived.

"Jonathan," she reproved him, "stop teasing Barbara at once. It's very unkind."

But Jonathan was beyond reason. He had begun by defying his

feeling of loneliness. He was ready now to defy the whole world. He wasn't going to be bossed by Aunt Joy, any more than he was going to be bossed by Barbara. He wasn't going to be bossed by anyone. He was so much excited that he didn't know what he was saying.

"You shut up!" he shouted, "I'm not going to be bossed by *you.*"

Rachel opened the door just in time to hear this.

"How *dare* you talk like that to Auntie Joy, Jonathan?" she said, breathlessly.

"I dare," he shouted excitedly. "I'm not frightened of any of you. I hate you all."

He kicked the waste-paper basket across the room as hard as he could. It knocked a bowl off a little table.

Dickie watched him fascinated. Rachel's eyes were bright with anger. This sort of thing always happened before Joy.

"You naughty boy," she said. "I'll tell your father the minute he gets in."

"He's growing very quickly," put in Joy, in a well-meaning attempt to smooth over the situation. "I always find that a little extra sleep's what they need when they get nervy like that."

Rachel's eyes grew brighter still, and she set her lips. That Joy should dare to insinuate that she didn't give her children enough sleep! What business was it of Joy's, anyway? Jonathan was worth twenty of Joy's well-behaved little sheep. She bundled the still weeping Barbara into her coat. Laura was crying, too, now. It was growing dark, and to go home they would have to pass the shop where dead little boys and girls stood in the window wearing party clothes. A boy at school had told Laura that they were dead little boys and girls, and that if you went past the shop after dark the man would come out and catch you, and kill you, and put you in his window with them. The thought of it never troubled her except when she had to pass the window after dark. Then it troubled her dreadfully, but she always forgot it as soon as she had safely passed it.

"She's tired," said Joy, collecting her little belongings.

It never occurred to Laura to tell Joy that she was afraid of being killed by the man who kept dead little boys and girls in his window. She thought that everyone knew that they were dead little boys and girls.

Jonathan sat slouched on one of the chairs in the hall, staring in front of him moodily, his hands in his pockets. .... He'd catch a disease and die, and then they'd remember how beastly they'd all been to him, and they'd be sorry, and it would serve them right.

Joy, putting on Laura's outdoor shoes, glanced across the room at Christopher. He hardly seemed to realise that they were there. He moved and spoke as if he were in a dream. He looked old and very tired. She felt a sudden aching pity for him.

Christopher looked up and caught her gaze fixed on him. His heart missed a beat, then began to race. What did her look mean? Did it mean that she knew, that they all knew? He came to a sudden decision. He would go to Frank to-morrow, tell him exactly what Susan had said, and ask him if he had ever had any suspicions or heard any rumours.

He could bear knowledge of the worst better than this heart-sickening uncertainty. He said "good-bye" to them abstractedly.

In the kitchen, Lydia was carefully storing away the cracker trimmings that she had found on the dining-room floor.

Chapter Fifteen

STEPHEN opened the front door, then stood in the hall for a minute listening. From the drawing-room came an eager buzz of voices that died away suddenly, leaving silence. Wanda played bridge in her own drawing-room, or some one else's, every day of her life. . . . He could see the inside of the room as well as if he had opened the door and looked in. Smartly dressed women like dolls with plucked eyebrows, reddened lips, and harsh un-softened brows, women so much alike that Stephen could hardly tell the difference between them. They were sitting at card-tables, their doll-like faces expressionless, but as tense, as rapacious, as predatory, as animals of prey. Wanda prided herself on belonging to Ravenham's only "smart set". Wanda had been beautiful when he married her, but she had so schooled her beauty into uniformity that there was, in Stephen's eyes, little of it left. She had impressed her personality upon the house, too, so that Stephen hated every room of it except his own study. He hated the drawing-room most of all, with the heap of crudely coloured cushions on the floor, and the grotesque dolls, as big as children, poised on the back of the couch and on the chairs.

He went slowly upstairs to his study. It was a pleasant room with a bay window overlooking the back garden. There were Persian rugs on a stained floor. The cream-coloured walls were hung with a few of his best prints in narrow black frames. His portfolio of prints stood against the wall. His small precious collection of first editions was in the locked Sheraton bookcase.

The fire was laid on the hearth. It was supposed to be lighted at half-past five, but when Wanda was giving a bridge party no one in the house had time for anything else. He put a light to it, and then stood, his hands in his pockets, his frowning gaze fixed on the floor. Wanda had been out when he came in from his talk with Olivia. She had rung him up at dinner time to say that she would not be back to dinner, and that he must not wait up for her. She had been still in bed when he went out this morning. He must speak to her now, as soon as these people had gone. Another burst of noise came from the drawing-room, then died away.

He sat in the arm-chair by the fire and glanced around the room. All his treasures, his prints, his first editions, his antiques, were bargains picked up for half their value after careful searching. He would sell them before he went away with Olivia. They would bring in enough to keep things going till he had time to look round. Olivia was not like Wanda. She would not want luxury, expensive things to wear, expensive things to eat, expensive things around her. But—there would still be Wanda.

Then a sudden vivid memory of Olivia blotted out everything else, and filled him with a sharp exultation, stirring his pulses so that he longed for nothing better than to fight and suffer for her. He was glad that things were not going to be too easy. He had sunk into a rut, but he was not old yet. He felt a great thankfulness that this love had come to him, bringing back his youth, jerking him from the path of easy-going cynical disillusion along which he had been drifting.

A gentle tap at the door roused him.

"Come in."

Clarissa opened the door very quietly, and stood for a minute on the threshold. She had thrown off her hat and coat in the hall. She wore a navy blue kilted skirt and a shantung blouse. Her chestnut curls were rumpled. She trailed a school satchel by its strap.

"May I come in, darling?"

Without waiting for an answer, she closed the door, and ran lightly across the room, sinking down on to the hearth-rug at his feet.

"I've been praying all the way from school that you'd be at home. It was hateful yesterday when you weren't."

She leaned her head against his knee, as she spoke, like an affectionate puppy, and his hand wandered to it, stroking the silky curls. Then she turned, raising her deep blue eyes to him, and her short upper lip lifted in a smile that showed small perfect teeth.

"Let's go to our land, shall we?" she said.

Their land was a secret magic land that they had invented. Extraordinary adventures happened to them in it. Sometimes Stephen made up the adventures, but more often Clarissa. Some of the inhabitants of the land were friendly, others were hostile, but, whenever Stephen was in danger, Clarissa rescued him, and, whenever Clarissa was in danger, Stephen rescued her. Witches and wizards and fauns and elves and gnomes were at every corner, strange fruits grew on strange trees, magic was everywhere, any animal they met might be a human being under a spell. Once Stephen had spent three days as a frog, whilst Clarissa had searched the land for a spell to turn him back to himself. Sometimes Stephen found himself inventing adventures in his office when his mind should have been intent on his work.

"Not to-night, dear," he said, absently.

She had spent yesterday evening, when he was away from home, making up an adventure to tell him to-night, but she did not protest. Her love for him gave her an unchildlike quickness of perception where he was concerned. She always knew instinctively when he wanted to be left alone.

"May I look at *Don Quixote?*" she whispered.

He nodded, and she slipped over to the bookcase, to drag out the huge volume of *Don Quixote* with Doré's illustrations. She laid it on the hearthrug and sat very still, turning over the pages one by one. She was never tired of looking at the pictures. She loved Sancho's ass so much that she often took it with her on her imaginary adventures.

Stephen's hand lay on his knees, and she turned her head suddenly to press her lips upon it. He had almost recaptured the mood she had disturbed, but at the touch of her lips—baby lips, clean and soft and fragrant as rose petals—the knowledge of her childish love crept in upon his thoughts of Olivia, like a discord, jarring them. He tried to hold his exultation, but it eluded him and vanished, leaving a heavy weariness and depression. He could not think of Olivia without thinking of Clarissa. Wanda ignored the child, except for a spasmodic interest in her clothes, and Stephen had long realised that Clarissa's sensitiveness shrank from the hardness that was Wanda's chief characteristic. They were so alien in temperament that there was little likelihood of the years bringing them nearer to each other. Already Wanda was irritated by the child, and Clarissa grew frightened and stupid beneath her irritation. He suspected that, without knowing it, she looked to him for protection against Wanda.

The door opened and a housemaid entered with a tray of tea, which she put on a small table by Stephen's chair.

"I'm sorry it's so late, sir," she said, "we've all been so busy downstairs."

"Have you had yours?" he said to Clarissa.

"I'm sorry, sir," said the maid, quickly on the defensive. "Madam left no orders. They've had theirs in the drawing-room, and the dining-room's all cluttered up with the furniture from the drawing-room, and I clean forgot about Miss Clarissa."

"Bring some up here for her," said Stephen.

So Clarissa sat cross-legged on the hearth-rug by her tray of milk, and bread and butter, and sponge cake, thrilling with delight.

After tea she washed her hands in the cupboard in the corner of the room that contained a hand basin and tap. It was one of her greatest treats to be allowed to wash her hands there. Then she sat on the hearth-rug again, and looked up at him half anxiously, as if sensing some vague trouble in him.

"Is it a nuisance having me here?" she said. "Would you like me to go away?"

He put his hand on the thin childish shoulder.

"No, stay and talk to me," he said.

"What shall I talk about?"

"Anything you like."

Her blue eyes, fixed on him, held a deep serenity of love and trust beneath their anxiety.

"Yesterday when you weren't here," she said, "I sat on your chair, and pretended I was on your knee, and made up an adventure for us just as if you were there. But it wasn't really nice. I couldn't pretend hard enough."

He wasn't listening. He was thinking: She'll soon forget; children soon forget.

"Will you show me your pictures?" she said, suddenly.

Her instinct was still trying to wean him from his strange absorption. He loved his pictures. Talking to her about them, he would forget his mysterious trouble. Already part of her was his mother. She drew him over to the portfolio, and switched on the light that was just above.

He had forgotten everything but his prints, when he heard the voices of departing guests upraised shrilly in the hall. All Wanda's friends had shrill voices.

"Where's your adorable baby, Wanda? I'd love to see her."

"I don't know where she is," answered Wanda carelessly. "She won't be fit to be seen anyway. She's probably got on one of those ghastly garments they call gym. tunics. I shan't take any interest in her till she's left school and can be decently clothed."

Clarissa unconsciously drew closer to him.

The voices died away to a few belated leave-takings.

"Good-bye, darling."

"Good-bye. . . . I'm ruined, but it's been a heavenly afternoon. You won't forget mine on Tuesday?"

Then silence.

"Go on looking at them for a minute by yourself," said Stephen. "I want to go down and speak to mother."

Wanda was standing in the middle of the empty drawing-room, repairing her make-up. She wore a black chiffon dress, with huge bell cuffs of crimson, and her black satin shoes had red heels. Her hair was the fashionable length, and arranged in the fashionable way, with a sleek unnatural-looking wave, that proclaimed itself a "permanent". Her eyebrows and lashes were darkened, her lips a streak of carmine. Her whole allure was deliberately artificial.

He closed the door behind him.

"I want to speak to you."

She raised her head, with her faintly malicious smile.

"There's nothing to stop you, is there?"

Then she shut up her make-up case with a snap, made her way gracefully through the card-tables to the cushion-heaped divan, and sank down upon it, lighting a cigarette.

Her hard, bright self-possession always put him at a disadvantage. He stood on the hearth-rug, looking on the floor for a few minutes. His lips were set, deepening the hollows in his cheeks. Then he raised his eyes slowly to hers.

"We've not made a particularly great success of our marriage, Wanda."

She smiled at him again through her cigarette smoke.

"You always had a genius for stating the obvious, Stephen. You've surely not come downstairs just to tell me that."

He looked about him. He disliked having to discuss this with her here among the chaos of card-tables, littered with cigarette ends and bonbon papers. The ghosts of the women who had sat at the little tables seemed to watch him from the corners of the room with hard, bright, malicious smiles like Wanda's. He spoke abruptly and with an effort.

"I want to tell you that I—love someone else."

She shrugged her shoulders.

"But why not? And why tell me? I've never interfered with you, have I? Please don't begin to be crude."

He was a man whose passions were not easily stirred, and he had never been unfaithful to her, but from the earliest days of their marriage she had taken his unfaithfulness for granted with a cynicism that had shocked him then inexpressibly. He stood looking at her in silence. She had been in the van of every changing fashion since he had known her, but he could still see in her traces of the girl he had fallen in love with, the deep blue eyes, the flawless skin, the small shapely head. She dyed her hair auburn now, but once it had been a golden chestnut like Clarissa's. They had been engaged within a fortnight of their first meeting and married within a month. He had been in love with her, but he had soon realised that it was his position rather than himself that had attracted her.

Throughout their engagement, and at the beginning of their married life, she had set herself deliberately to charm him, to make him see in her everything that he wished to see, pretending a hundred interests that she did not feel. She had tired of it soon enough after marriage, and his gradual disillusionment had begun. His love had died so completely that it left no trace at all behind it, only a faint memory as of something incredible. He had been intolerably lonely till a few years ago, when Clarissa—very sweet and shy, with nothing of Wanda about her but her beauty—began to fill the emptiness. And now this new love had come, radiating warmth and light through his heart, setting his pulses afire, bringing back his youth.

"I've never been unfaithful to you," he said. "I'm not going to be unfaithful now in the sense that I'm not going to enter on an intrigue here in Ravenham. I'm going to leave you openly."

Her eyes narrowed and grew watchful, but her lips were still curved into the malicious smile he hated.

"How adorably Victorian of you to talk about unfaithfulness, Stephen."

"Will you divorce me?"

"Why should I divorce you?"

"I want to marry her."

"Why? Surely the thing can be arranged without that?"

"It can't be arranged without that," he said shortly.

She laughed.

"She's very particular, isn't she?"

Then she took out a comb and mirror from her bag and began to comb back her hair, completely absorbed in the task. As he watched her a sudden gust of hatred shook him. He wanted to throw aside the self-control of years and shout abuse at her. Words that he had never used in his life crowded to his lips. He turned away and stood with his back to her, moving the ornaments on the mantelpiece to and fro with unsteady fingers. Then he turned to her again and said quietly:

"Well?"

"What do you mean by 'well'?" she said, as she studied her reflection with an abstracted frown.

"Will you divorce me?"

She shut up her case and put it back into her bag.

"Once again, why should I?"

"I shall leave you in any case."

"My dear Stephen, I haven't the slightest objection to being a grass widow. An absent husband is quite an enviable possession. I should go to London and live at an hotel. I've always wanted to. I should live my own life in my own way. But I prefer to have a husband present or absent."

"Very well," he said, "I can only repeat that I shall go away all the same."

She turned on him with a sudden flicker of anger and contempt.

"You talk like a child. Can't you arrange this thing without making a fool of yourself and me? Who is this woman?"

"That doesn't matter."

"It does matter. Don't you see that she's trying to ruin you? If she doesn't live in Ravenham, surely she can come here."

"We won't discuss that, please."

"You'll have to continue to support me."

"I'm quite aware of that."

She leaned forward to stub the end of her cigarette on an ash-tray on one of the card-tables, and spoke in her usual, slightly drawling tones.

"The woman is either very clever or a perfect fool. Is she anyone I know?"

He flushed hotly.

"I've already told you," he said evenly, "that we won't discuss her."

She yawned, then slowly rose from the divan.

"Well," she said, "I think we've settled everything, haven't we? You're going to leave me and I'm not going to divorce you. The situation is quite simple. I'm going up to change now. The maids will want to put this room straight."

She had reached the door, when he said suddenly, "Wait a minute, please. There's something else."

She turned and looked at him with cool calculating eyes. "Yes?"

He hesitated, as if uncertain how to begin, and finally said: "You can't possibly live at a hotel with Clarissa."

"Why not? Lots of children live at hotels."

"You must see that it is a most unsuitable life for a child."

"On the contrary, it's good for them. They meet people. They get poise."

He laughed shortly.

"Poise! . . . Good God!"

"Was that all you wanted to say?"

"No "

"Well?"

He spoke stumblingly, without looking at her. "I take it that you'll have no objection to my having Clarissa for part of the year at any rate?"

A glint of malicious triumph came into her eyes, and her lips curved into their hard bright smile.

"Why should I let you have Clarissa?"

"I'm her father."

"You surely don't expect me to make things easy for you."

"You've already said that my leaving you will cause you no inconvenience—that you'll be free to live your own life in your own way."

"But that won't alter the fact that you'll have left me. . . ." The mocking lights in her eyes grew brighter. "I couldn't let my child visit a man who was living in open immorality. Any respectable person would support me in that."

He controlled his anger with difficulty.

"You know that Clarissa means more to me than she can ever mean to you. Would you seriously prevent my ever seeing her again just out of spite?"

"Not spite, Stephen, dear. Respectability. I shall be solely responsible for her upbringing if you leave me, and I must be very careful of her. I couldn't possibly let her go into equivocal surroundings or meet equivocal people."

His hands trembled. He wanted to take her throat in his two hands and choke the devil's mockery out of it. Through a sudden mist he still heard her mocking voice.

"You really ought to be grateful to me, you know. Lots of men would give their eyes to have a *femme complaisante*. I've always thought divorce such a silly idea. Tell your mistress that from me, will you?"

He heard the door shut, then the sound of her light, drawling voice as she gave orders to a maid in the hall.

Chapter Sixteen

FRANK looked up from the letter he was reading.

"This is from old Dobbin. Do you remember him?"

"No," said Rachel, shortly.

For several days now her temper had been serene, but he had realised early this morning that the serenity had left it. All the time that they were dressing, her silences and short answers had challenged him to give her an excuse for recounting her grievances by asking what was the matter.

"I knew him at Guy's," he went on. "He was at our wedding."

"I don't remember him."

Her tone and look still proclaimed her unhappiness, begged him to notice it, to comment on it, to offer consolation, to assure her of his love.

"He's motoring through Ravenham to-day, and wants to call on us. He says he'll be here by four. Will that be all right?"

He rather overdid the cheerfulness and casualness of his voice. He was anxious to get away from her before the storm broke. Sitting there, telling her with overdone cheerfulness about Dobbin, he was like a little boy running from a half-glimpsed bogy.

"Yes. I'm going to lunch with Violet, but I shall be back by four."

"That's splendid. I suppose he can stay the night if he can manage it."

"Of course."

He laid down his table napkin and went from the room whistling. His whistling defied the pregnant silence that surrounded her. He reached the door with a sense of escape, and went to the consulting-room. He was glad to see that there were already several patients in the waiting-room. She could not follow him there, and he need not go back to the other part of the house before setting out on his rounds. Part of him felt remorseful, and longed to go back to comfort her, the other part—the part that shrank from her emotion and feared its effect on his work—felt as if relieved of a heavy weight.

In the dining-room the two children ate their breakfast in silence. Barbara's placidity was impervious to any emotional currents in the atmosphere, but Jonathan was as sensitive to Rachel's moods as his father, and as anxious to escape from them.

"May I go, please, Mummy?" He slipped from his chair and went to the door, his eye fixed on her warily as he passed her, lest she should snatch him up and kiss him, as she sometimes did when that look was on her face.

Barbara was left alone, eating her bread and treacle with slow deliberation. When she had finished it, Rachel took her upstairs to wash her hands and get her ready for school. Barbara was distrait because Brenda had pneumonia, and the crisis was due to-day.

"You'll look after her, Mummy, won't you?"

"Yes. You love Brenda, don't you?"

"Yes."

"And you love poor Mummy just a little bit, don't you?"

"Yes," said Barbara, in an absent fashion that gave a twist to the knife in Rachel's heart.

Rachel went downstairs with her.

"Where's Jonathan?" she said.

"He's gone," volunteered the maid who was dusting the hall.

Rachel bit her lip. He had gone, like Frank, without even saying good-bye. They *hated* her, both of them. . . .

"Say good-bye nicely to Mummy, Barbara, darling."

She clasped Barbara in a long embrace. Barbara endured it restively. She had not any objection to being kissed, but Jonathan had gone to school without her, and she did not want to be late. She wriggled out of Rachel's arms and set off at a run down the road, hoping to catch up Jonathan before he reached school.

Rachel went upstairs and began to turn out drawers in her bedroom with feverish energy, marshalling in a sort of ghostly array all the people who hated her. Frank, first of all, who didn't care how unhappy she was, and went off without even saying good-bye to her. . . . Jonathan, who had gone to school without kissing her. . . . Barbara, who had wriggled impatiently out of her embrace. . . . Joy, who was jealous of her children, and told her in public that she didn't give them enough sleep. . . . Frank's father, who openly humiliated her by his affectionate manner to Olivia. . . . Olivia, with her maddening air of aloofness, avoiding her whenever she could. . . . Mrs. Dunton, who had asked her to her second bridge drive instead of her first. . . . Mrs. Handley, who had asked Violet to bring her to tea, instead of ringing up and asking her in person. . . . Mrs. Marret, who had told her that a book she had praised was badly written. . . . Mrs. Templeton, who had passed her in the car without offering her a lift. . . . Mrs. Mostin, who had spoken to her in the town, but had not introduced her to her mother, who was with her. . . . Mrs. Chester, who had passed her in North Street without looking at her. . . . Mrs. Lawson, who had not asked Barbara to Rosemary's birthday party. . . . Her mother, who had not written to her for three weeks, and then had written a letter full of her own concerns, not showing the faintest interest in her daughter's. . . . Even the maid, who had said, "He's gone," openly exulting in Jonathan's unkindness.

The list grew until it included everyone in the world, because, if everyone who knew her hated her, naturally all the others would hate her if they knew her.

Unable to contain herself any longer, she slammed the drawer she was tidying, and flung herself on to her bed in a tempest of tears. Through her tears she heard the sound of Frank's car starting up as he set off on his rounds. He knew that she was unhappy, but he didn't care. He had never even asked her what was the matter. He hated her, probably he would be glad if she died. As usual, only one part of her lay sobbing on the bed, the other part stood by, watching, racked with pity. . . . Her crying brought on a headache, and that made her feel better, because the pain distracted her attention from the worldful of people who hated her. She rose slowly from the bed, bathed her face and hands in cold water, and began to get ready to go to Violet's.

Violet's house had either an exhilarating or depressing effect on Rachel according to her mood. Often, when she set off for her own home feeling quite cheerful, depression would seize her as soon as she entered Violet's spacious hall, with the deep carpets, masses of flowers, antique furniture, and general air of expensiveness. And often, on the other hand, when she left home feeling gloomy, the quiet luxury of the beautiful surroundings would vaguely soothe and cheer her. And so now, as she leant back in the most comfortable chair in Violet's pretty drawing-room, with the October sunshine filtering through net curtains, and Violet fussing about her solicitously, relieving her of her things, bringing a footstool for her feet, her mercurial spirits swung up from the depth, and she forgot even her headache. Violet, watching with loving anxiety, felt the radiant happiness that she had felt throughout her childhood and girlhood when Rachel was in a good temper. The two of them laughed and chattered like a pair of schoolgirls. All the things that had seemed so terrible to Rachel only an hour ago were terrible no longer. They laughed uproariously over Mrs. Dunton's second evening bridge party.

"It was too funny for words," said Rachel. "She hadn't even bothered to keep the sandwiches fresh. They were dry and curled up, quite obviously the left-overs from the night before. And there were little dishes of jelly, with honestly little more than a scraping in."

The naughtiness of Barbara and Jonathan, which had worried her so this morning, suddenly became funny too.

"And when Barbara went to the tin where she keeps her ants' eggs for the gold fish she found it empty. Jonathan had *eaten* a whole packet of ants' eggs. He said he was hungry and liked the taste."

"The monkey!"

"Barbara was awfully upset, because it was early closing day, and she couldn't get any more. Poor Barbara, she had a very bad day yesterday. She'd eaten some grapes with all the pips, and Jonathan kept telling her that he could see a vine beginning to grow out of her mouth. But he was sorry when he saw that she was really frightened, and gave her one of his marbles."

"Aren't they *ducks*?" said Violet happily, and added, "I think they're *heaps* nicer than Joy's children."

And Rachel, her heart glowing warmly, said, "Oh, but Joy's are darlings, too."

"They're all right," agreed Violet, "but they haven't the *character* of Jonathan and Barbara. . . . How's Frank?"

"Very busy. This morning, for instance, he had to dash off from his consulting-room to his rounds without coming in to see me at all."

And, as she spoke, her heart was full of loving pity for poor old Frank, who hadn't even time to run in and see her between his consulting hours and his rounds.

Then Violet showed her the letter that she had received last night from their mother. It was just like the one Rachel had received, full of excited comments on the visitors at the hotel where she lived, of descriptions of her new autumn clothes, and her latest bridge party.

"Isn't it absurd?" laughed Violet affectionately. "How *can* she think it will interest us to know what sort of bridge hands people whom we've never seen and never will see, had at her party."

Mrs. Elleston, their mother, had been left a widow when Violet was only a few months old. She was a good-natured, rather stupid, woman, who saw everyone and everything through rose-coloured spectacles, and whose guiding principle in life it was to avoid unpleasantness of any sort. Rachel had been a stormy, self-willed child, and it was easier to yield to her than to stand out against her. Therefore Mrs Elleston had always yielded to her. The household was miserable when Rachel was in one of her "moods", and happy when Rachel was happy, and so Mrs Elleston, for the sake of her own comfort, took a good deal of pains to keep Rachel happy, giving her the most important place in the little family circle, arranging treats for her, buying her presents, flattering her, repeating to her every compliment that she heard paid to her, and even, when Rachel's "mood" was hovering near, inventing them. She had pandered ceaselessly and shamelessly to Rachel's egotism, and in doing so saw herself as a perfect mother, devoted and unselfish. Rachel had artistic talents slightly above the average, and her mother had early decided to look on her as a genius, chiefly because that bestowed on her a sort of licence to indulge in moods unchecked. She had been a sallow angular child, but adolescence had brought her a fitful beauty that had ripened and matured with the years. As her figure lost the angularity of her childhood, it had become full, firm, and seductively graceful, while her sallowness had changed to a clear pallor that held a kind of glow as if lit by a light within. Her lips were soft and red and full, her eyes lustrous and heavily fringed.

The younger sister's beauty was of a different kind, and she had altered very little with the years. At the age of twenty-five she still had the same childish blue eyes, wistful mouth, and a pink and white skin, that she had had when she was five. She was as good natured as and even more stupid than her mother. There had been a certain amount of conscious self-deception about Mrs. Elleston's cult of Rachel's "genius", and Rachel herself only believed in it when her blackest moods of self pity were upon her, but Violet had accepted the legend unquestioningly, and from childhood had adored Rachel blindly. There could have been no worse atmosphere for Rachel to grow up in than her mother's lazy spoiling, and Violet's adoration. As she emerged from adolescence, her moods became more wearing, and, when she married Frank Mainwaring, her mother had felt a relief that she confided to no one, least of all herself. She wept unremittingly and quite sincerely throughout the wedding ceremony, then she married Violet off as quickly as she could to the richest man she could find, and, with a glow of conscious virtue, seeing herself as a mother who had nobly performed her duty to the uttermost, left Ravenham, and went to live at a hotel in Bournemouth.

John Morgan, Violet's husband, was an uneducated middle-aged manufacturer, who cherished the Victorian belief that women should be guarded, and protected, and shielded from all the unpleasantness of life. Violet, essentially a Victorian woman in her outlook on life, was very happy with him. The only shadow on her happiness was the fact that her husband did not appreciate Rachel.

To-day Rachel's mood of radiant happiness lasted through lunch (perfectly cooked, perfectly served), and throughout the afternoon, and Violet sunned herself in her kindness, worshipping her with the old fervent adoration.

They walked round the garden, arm in arm, in the autumn sunshine. Violet picked a bunch of chrysanthemums for her from the hot-house, and they chattered gaily of friends and acquaintances, with this precious (because precarious) feeling of happy intimacy between them.

"How's poor old Mr. Mainwaring?" said Violet at last.

"He's much better," said Rachel. "He went for a motor tour in Somerset, you know, to take his mind off things, and it did him a lot of good. We all do our best to keep the poor old man cheerful, of course."

And, as she spoke, she saw a happy united family—she and Frank, Joy and Bruce, Derek and Olivia—all doing their best to keep the poor old man cheerful.

"He's lucky to have you," said Violet, and she put a slight accent on the "you", so that Rachel saw herself as the old man's favourite daughter-in-law, saw his kindness to Olivia as goodness of heart, because he didn't want Olivia to feel left out in the cold.

"He's a darling," she said happily.

Then John came home, stocky, slow, rather stern – looking, with the unmistakable hint of Cockney in his manner and accent, and everything was spoilt.

The instinctive hostility between him and Rachel leapt out as soon as their eyes met. That Rachel was obviously making Violet happy this afternoon, did not lessen her brother-in-law's resentment, but rather increased it. She could do it so easily, and she chose to do it so seldom. And, as he greeted her with his slightly ironic smile, Rachel felt her happiness slipping from her, though she clutched at it desperately. How *could* Violet be happy with this boor?

She rose.

"I must go now, Vi."

"Won't you stay to tea?" pleaded Violet.

"No thanks," said Rachel, "I can't possibly. There's the children's tea to see to, and a friend of Frank's is coming."

With the fading of her elation and excitement, the old desire to torment returned to her.

"I shall have to put on an apron, and make the bread and butter as soon as I get in. It's Polly's afternoon out. I shall probably be dropping by to-night."

She hated John for the smile with which he said good-bye to her.

At home she took off her things, lit the fire in the drawing-room, and began to get tea for the children in the dining-room. As she was crossing the hall with a jug of milk in one hand, and a plate of bread and butter in the other, Frank came in with his father, whom he had met entering the gate.

"How are you, my dear?" said Christopher, gently, as if he felt the heaviness of her spirit and were trying to propitiate her.

"I'm quite all right, thanks," she said.

She wanted to speak kindly to him, but, despite her efforts, her tone was curt and ungracious. Her depression redoubled as she turned away abruptly.

The two men entered the drawing-room, and stood over the chilly fire, holding out their hands to it.

Frank glanced at his father curiously, wondering why he had come. He was not in the habit of paying informal visits. Poor old man ... he was beginning to look his age. Getting rather prosy, too—meandering on about the weather and the government, and what ought to be done with the old Town Hall that stood like a derelict shipwreck in the middle of the town.

Christopher was talking absently, hardly knowing what he said.

He had come determined to tell Frank everything, but now that he was here it was unaccountably difficult. Whenever he tried to approach the subject, his heart began to beat unevenly, and he swerved off on to something else. "He never used to be like this," thought Frank. "He seems ten years older since Mother died."

"Frank," said Christopher suddenly, "just before your mother died, she said something about Charles Barrow. You remember him, don't you?"

"Uncle Charlie? Yes, of course, I do. Jolly old blighter, wasn't he? I remember him quite well. What did she say about him?"

Christopher drew a deep breath. Frank was as ingenuous as a child. If he had known anything he would have betrayed it in look or tone. . . .

"I don't know," said Christopher. "I couldn't catch it. I just heard his name."

Frank nodded understandingly. "Her mind had gone back to the old days," he said. "It often does."

Frank had always been rather obtuse, thought Christopher. He would, perhaps, be the last person to know a thing like that.

Derek? Derek was too self-centred to see anything that did not concern himself. Women had sharper eyes than men. Joy might know. He would ask Joy to-morrow.

The children came in from school, and Barbara brought Brenda for him to examine and pronounce out of danger. Frank had long since refused to treat Brenda.

"She's going to have appendicitis next," said Barbara in a business-like tone of voice.

"I took her appendix out myself," said Frank, "the first year you had her."

"I know, it's grown again," said Barbara.

"Do you spend the whole of your time at school thinking out what diseases Brenda's going to have next?"

"I do sometimes. I didn't to-day. To-day I was thinking about the house I'm going to live in when I'm grown up."

"And what sort of house are you going to live in when you grow up?" said Christopher.

"Very, very big," said Barbara, "each room's going to be as big as a house, and there's going to be a sweet shop in one of the rooms, and a dressmaker's in the other, so that I can always have little bits of stuff."

"That's splendid," said Christopher vaguely. "Well, I must be off."

Poor old chap, thought Frank. He came for something, and now he's forgotten what he came for. He's beginning to break up.

He said good-bye absently, and Frank went down to the gate with him. As he was watching him walk slowly away, Dobbin's car drew up. Dobbin had changed from a slender, impudent youth into a confident, prosperous-looking man, with the genial manner that takes its welcome for granted. He greeted Frank affectionately.

"Well, old man, it's splendid to see you again. You didn't mind my barging in on you, I hope?"

Frank led him into the hall, where he greeted Rachel with the same high-spirited camaraderie. Rachel sent their tea into the drawing-room, and gave the children theirs in the dining-room.

From the drawing-room came the sound of the two men's voices, punctuated by shouts of laughter from Frank. The sound brought an obscure pain to Rachel's heart. She settled the children with their home work, then took her sewing into the drawing-room. The two men greeted her politely, but quite obviously she did not exist for them. They were back in their student days, living over old scenes, following up old friends. Frank had changed, the years had dropped from him. He was not a husband exhausted by his wife's demands, a father harassed by the expenses of a young family, a professional man watching with dismay a gradually diminishing practice. He was an undergraduate, and the world—a colossal joke—lay before him.

"Do you remember——?"

"Do you remember——?"

His laugh, whole-hearted, care-free, rang out again and again.

As Rachel sat, her head bent over her sewing, the obscure pain at her heart deepened, sharpened. Where she loved, it was torture to her not to possess and possess wholly. And now she knew that, during all these years when she thought she had possessed Frank, part of him had eluded her. She had never known this high-spirited, care-free boy. He did not belong to her. He was Frank, but he did not belong to her, and would never belong to her.

Suddenly she could endure it no longer, and, going abruptly from the room, began to busy herself over the preparation of the spare room for the guest, who had accepted their invitation to stay the night. The children were in bed long before she had finished, and she went in to say good night to them. She went to Jonathan first. He was sitting up in bed, his hands round his knees, his eyes fixed dreamily into the distance.

She sat down on his bed.

"What are you thinking of, darling?"

A guarded look came into his sharp, Puck's face.

"Nothing," he said, shortly.

The knife was drawn slowly out of her heart and plunged relentlessly into another place. A secret alien life was springing up in him—a life in which she had no part. His baby dependence on her was over. He had already secret dreams, secret hopes and fears, which he hugged jealously to himself. Already he was swaggering away from her along the road of life, not even looking back. And Barbara would follow him.

She had a sudden vivid memory of their babyhood . . . tiny arms outstretched to her, clasped tightly round her neck. They had looked to her for everything then. She had been their whole world. Frank, too, had been different in those days.

She thought of Frank sitting downstairs, talking eagerly to his friend of things and people of which she knew nothing, wholly absorbed in them, not caring whether she were there or not.

Frank took his friend to the spare bedroom, then went slowly to his own room. His spirit dropped lower at every step. He was still a carefree student when he said good night to Dobbin, but by the time he reached his door his normal worried state had closed upon him again.

A scene with Rachel had been brewing ever since early morning.

He had staved it off during the day, but he had to face it now. She would have innumerable imaginary grievances against him, and his friends, and everybody she knew. He would have to reason with her, argue with her, reassure her, calm her . . . and he was tired.

He opened the door. She was standing by the dressing-table in her night-dress. She turned to him as he entered, and the thought came to him that he had never seen her look more beautiful. Her dark eyes were shining, her cheeks softly flushed, her red passionate lips curved into a smile. There was a sort of glow, a radiance, about her whole body.

He closed the door behind him, and stood looking at her. As their eyes met, an exaltation of happiness, almost greater than she could bear, seized her.

"Frank," she said, "there isn't any reason why we shouldn't have another baby, is there?"

Chapter Seventeen

"You remember him, don't you?" said Christopher.

Joy was sitting near the window where she could see the bend in the road round which Miss Nash would appear with the children, coming home from their afternoon walk. She hated these autumn afternoons, when the mist began to come up soon after three. And Billy had been coughing last night. . . .

"Yes, I remember," she said, absently. "We used to call him Uncle Charlie."

It was nice of Father to come to see her, but really—Uncle Charlie, and the holidays they had spent with him at Selsey, and the time she and Mother had gone to his house for a pageant . . . it was *years* ago. How *could* he expect her to pretend to be interested in it? He had not even mentioned the children or Bruce. She had shown him the kettle-holder that Laura had made at school (it was very good indeed for a child of four), and he had hardly looked at it. He would persist in talking about things that had happened years ago, things that she had completely forgotten, and did not even want to remember. Uncle Charlie—a rather silly, stoutish man, who was always making jokes. She had heard that old people forgot the present and remembered things in the past that everyone else had forgotten long ago, but somehow she had not thought that that would happen to Father. He had always seemed so alert, so young. Mother's death had aged him a lot, of course. One must try to be patient with him. Still—he might have made some comment on Laura's kettle-holders. She did feel a little hurt about that.

"He came down every week-end one summer. Do you remember?"

"I believe he did," said Joy, trying hard to keep the impatience out of her voice and turning her head so as to see a little further round the bend. Yes, they were coming now—Miss Nash with the pram, Laura walking on one side of it, pushing her toy pram, and Billy on the other with his scooter. Her spirits soared up as innumerable heavy weights dropped from it. They had not had an accident. Bobs, quite obviously, had not fallen out of the pram on to her head and been killed while Miss Nash was in a shop. Billy had not been run over. Laura was not lost or kidnapped. . . . There was only Dickie now, and Dickie would be setting off from school in a few minutes. She would soon have them all with her again, warmly sheltered under her wing. Laura was waving her hand to the window, and running on in front of the others.

"She's seen you," said Joy. "Isn't she a darling?" and then, with a slight reproach in her voice, "Miss Golding said that that kettle-holder was extraordinarily well done for a child of her age."

Christopher followed her into the hall, where Miss Nash was edging the pram through the narrow front door. The children were rosy-cheeked with the fresh air. Billy had filled his pockets with conkers, which he proudly displayed to Christopher. Bobs stared at Christopher in solemn surprise, then ejaculated "G'andad," with sudden sharp emphasis, and wrinkled up her nose in a friendly grin. Miss Nash was brightly discoursive to Christopher, as she lifted the gaitered Bobs out of the pram, and gathered up an armful of wraps.

"You would have laughed, Mr. Mainwaring. I said to Billy, 'If you hadn't left your coat lying on the floor, poor Laura wouldn't have fallen over it,' and he said: 'Yes, but if I hadn't left it on the floor, she wouldn't have had something nice and soft to fall on.' "

Miss Nash was always particularly vivacious with "poor Mr. Mainwaring". She could not help feeling that it did him good and cheered him up to have a little talk with her.

Joy knows nothing, thought Christopher. She married Bruce straight from school, and she's as much a child now as when she married him. She knows nothing of the world. She wouldn't see a thing like that if it was thrust under her very nose. She's like a little girl fussing over her dolls.

"You'd better be getting Bobs upstairs, hadn't you, Miss Nash?" said Joy, kindly, but wishing that Miss Nash would stop chattering to Father in that irritating fashion.

"Of course, I must," beamed Miss Nash. "Say 'bye-bye' to Grandad nicely, darling."

Bobs said "bye-bye" nicely, and Miss Nash took her upstairs, still talking animatedly over her shoulder to Christopher till they had disappeared round the bend on to the landing. The other two were pulling at his arms, both talking at once.

"And yesterday he'd forgotten to bring his biscuits," shouted Billy, "and so I said I'd give him mine if he'd give me his two-hundred conker, and he gave it me, and then the next day he brought me some biscuits and wanted his two-hundred conker back, and I wouldn't give it him. I said it was just as if we were both starving for water in the desert, and he gave me a thousand pounds for my last drop of water, and then afterwards, when we were saved and back in England, he brought me a drop of water and wanted his thousand pounds back. I said it was like that. It *was*, wasn't it?"

"Billy, darling, don't shout so," said Joy.

"Let *me* talk to Grandad," said Laura passionately. "No one ever lets *me* talk."

"All right, you can talk to him now," said Billy indulgently.

"Grandad, I thought of a great big tiger when I was asleep in the night. A great big *suge* tiger."

"You mean you *dreamed*, Laura," said Billy. "It's dreaming when you're asleep."

"Don't worry Grandad, children," said Joy. "Run up and wash your hands for tea now. Won't you stay to tea, Father?"

"No, thank you, my dear," said Christopher. "I must be getting back now. Lydia will have my tea ready."

She felt a sudden compunction.

"Does Lydia look after you properly?"

"Oh yes, she's very good to me."

He would ask Olivia. Olivia would know. He thought of her eyes, shadowed, rather sad. It would be easier to ask her, too, than it had been to ask the others. He would go to Olivia.

Joy stood at the door till he had reached the gate. As he turned to close it, and to raise his hat, she smiled and waved to him, but her gaze wandered anxiously down the street. It was time that Dickie came. . . .

She went back slowly to the dining-room, where tea was laid, and stood looking at the table to see that nothing had been forgotten. The jug of milk, the bread and butter, the jam and honey, and the plain sponge cake. She thought suddenly of her own childhood, saw herself sitting at the dining-room table with Frank and Derek. Mother was at the head, smiling, cheerful, ready to laugh away incipient quarrels, to charm incipient tempers back to good humour. It was a long time since she had such a vivid memory of Mother. Mother. . . . She had made their childhood a very happy one. She had been tactful, understanding, full of a radiant serenity. She had passed over minor sulks, ignored little disobediences. You couldn't provoke a scene with her by naughtiness however hard you tried. And so you had never wanted to be naughty with her. Joy realised now, for the first time, that it was this atmosphere of serenity that she had been unconsciously trying to reproduce in her own home.

She went to the window again. Why was Dickie so late? She drew Bobs's high chair nearer to the table, then went upstairs to help Billy and Laura get ready for tea. Soon they were all downstairs, washed, and brushed, and shiningly clean. Bobs looked adorable, her straight, fair hair brushed like a boy's from her round smiling face, her legs emerging sturdy and dimpled from her clean rompers.

"Din-din!" she cried, excitedly, as she saw the tea-table. "Bobs' din-din!"

Billy murmured, "Tea, Bobs," but the correction was half-hearted. He had his hands full with Laura's education. He really couldn't undertake Bobs's as well.

"Mr. Mainwaring doesn't look himself," said Miss Nash.

"No," said Joy "and he could talk of nothing but things that had happened years ago and people I can hardly remember."

"They always get like that," said Miss Nash wisely. "It's old age. We won't wait for Dickie, will we?"

"No, he'll be here any minute," said Joy. "He's generally here before now, isn't he?"

Her eyes were fixed anxiously on the gate where Dickie's small, grey-clad figure should appear.

Dickie was walking through the town with Ralph. Ralph was the same age as Dickie, and sat next to him in school. They often walked home from school together. Ralph had found a stone in the school grounds and was taking it home with him. It was a large smooth stone the size of a well-grown potato. Ralph thought that its likeness to a potato gave it the character of a curio, and he had just started a museum in a cupboard at home, to which anything that he considered interesting was admitted.

"I shouldn't be a bit surprised," he said, "if it was some sort of a fossil. All sorts of things get fossilized, and this is probably some sort of fossilized potato."

They discussed this till the subject palled, then Ralph said, "Catch," and threw the stone to Dickie. Dickie caught it and returned it. They walked on, throwing and catching the stone. It was rather a good way of beguiling the journey. They came to the centre of the town, but the pavements were fairly clear, and they continued the game.

Then—it happened so quickly that Dickie could hardly realize it at first. He threw the stone to Ralph. Ralph, who was walking next the shop window, put out his hands to catch it and missed it. There was a clatter of breaking glass, and Ralph, after one terrified glance around him, disappeared. Dickie stood motionless, paralysed by terror. People were crowding round. An angry woman had come out of the shop and was shouting at him. He didn't hear any of the words she said. He heard nothing but a dull roaring that seemed to fill the whole world, he saw nothing but a thick mist that covered everything around him. His throat was dry, and the palms of his hands were sticky. His heart was banging like a gun. This was the end. They'd take him to prison now. They'd keep him there in a cell for years and years. He'd never see Mummy, or Daddy, or Billy, or Laura, or Bobs again. A policeman was making his way through the crowd. The woman was still shouting, "I'd take the skin off your back if you was mine—I'd learn you."

"What's all this?" said the policeman.

"This lad threw a stone at her window," explained one of the crowd.

The policeman was young and self-important. He looked from the broken window to the small boy who stood staring at him with a white expressionless face.

"Now, my lad," he said sharply, "you can't go about doing this sort of thing." He took out his notebook, "I want your name and address."

Through the black despair of Dickie's heart shot a ray of hope. They didn't know who he was. Perhaps they couldn't put him in prison without knowing who he was.

"I'll have to go and see your father about this," went on the policeman.

Perhaps they couldn't put you in prison without telling your father. He thought quickly. He'd rather go to Hell when he died for telling a lie than go to prison now.

"Albert Jones," he said, in a small, unsteady voice, "and I live at 31 High Street."

The policeman began to write it down in his book.

Dickie looked round warily. Yes, there was a thin place just there in the crowd. He'd dash out by it suddenly, while the policeman was still writing in his book, and run home so fast that they wouldn't know where he'd gone.

But a woman in the crowd said suddenly, "Why, it's one of the little Rangers."

"Eh?" said the policeman. "What's that?"

"It's Dickie Ranger. He lives in Elmwood Road."

The policeman looked at Dickie, shocked by this further proof of his depravity.

"Here, you know," he said solemnly, "this won't do either—giving false names and addresses. Why——"

But Dickie had darted through the thin place in the crowd, and was already vanishing round a corner, and down a back-street. He ran till he could run no longer, then he stopped, and leant panting against a wall. There was a sharp pain in his side, but he was hardly conscious of it. The street where he found himself was one he had never been in before, dingy and ill-lighted, little more than an alley between the backs of two rows of squalid houses. He stood listening intently for a moment. No one was running after him. He began to think what he must do next. He couldn't go home, of course, ever again. The policeman knew where he lived now, and he would always be there waiting to take him to prison. Mummy had said that mothers and fathers couldn't stop them from taking you to prison if you broke the law. He'd broken the law, and so he would have to go to prison if the policeman caught him. He saw again the picture in his story-book of the dark cell, with bars at the tiny window high in the wall, saw himself with heavy irons on his feet, rags hanging on his body, a rat watching him from a corner.

A clock struck five. He had a sudden vision of them sitting round the tea-table at home ... the warm, bright room, Mummy at one end of the table, Miss Nash at the other, Bobs in her high chair, Billy and Laura ... all talking and laughing together. Mummy smiling and trying to listen to them all at once. Sometimes Bobs got excited, and screwed up her face to make them laugh. Perhaps she was doing that now. The thought that he would never see them again was more than he could bear. He leant against the wall, his head on his arm, and sobbed desolately. It had begun to rain, a thin drizzle that changed quickly to a heavy downpour. He stood there in the dark back-street, his small figure shaken by the convulsive heart-broken sobs of childhood. He thought of Mummy tucking him in at night, her arm about him, her warm kiss on his cheek ... and his heart almost broke. Then he roused himself. He must go on. He mustn't be anywhere where the policeman could find him. He'd walk on, and on, and on, till he got to the coast, and then he'd go to sea. He'd often read in story books about boys who ran away and went to sea. His throat and head were aching with crying, but still he couldn't stop. He began to stumble on in the rain through the warren of back-streets. He must hurry. ...

Whatever happened, the policeman mustn't find him. His sodden clothes clung to him. The water was running down his back. He heard a clock strike six. Mummy would be giving Bobs her bath. Often they all helped to give Bobs her bath, because Bobs was so sweet and funny in it. His fear and misery overcame him again, and he sank down suddenly on to the pavement, a small, sodden, sobbing heap of misery. A wave of physical sickness swept over him. Perhaps he was going to die. It would be horrible to die in this dark street. Then there came a faint far-away strain of music. It seemed to stretch out friendly fingers through the darkness, comforting, beckoning. His sobs died away, and he got up and went slowly in the direction of the sound. It led him into another street, a dingy little street, with a row of squalid, badly-lighted shops. One of them was a gramophone shop, and the sound came from there.

It was a raucous enough sound, but to Dickie it was indescribably consoling. He hovered in the doorway. An old man in his shirt sleeves, wearing carpet slippers, was putting away some records behind the counter. He peered short-sightedly at the small, soaked figure with the swollen, tear-stained face, and said, "Come in, sonny, and listen if you like. It's a good tune, ain't it?"

Then he shuffled his way into an inner room. The kindness of his tone lay like a benediction on the child's spirit, stilling his terror and despair. He entered the shop, and stood there listening to the lilting old-fashioned strains of *The Blue Danube*. Somehow the music made him think of Gran, and he felt a sudden, passionate longing for her. She was always kind, and she was never frightened. Mummy was always kind, but she was frightened as well. You felt it always there behind her kindness. She was frightened of dreadful things happening to you, and it made you frightened too. Gran was never frightened. She would not have been frightened even now. A sudden memory of her face came to him, so vivid that it was as if he saw her there in the shop with him. Her eyes were laughing, tender. She wasn't shocked or frightened. She said, "You little silly! Run home this minute." He could hear her saying it through the music. All his fear and unhappiness left him suddenly. He felt as if he had awakened from a bad dream.

The record died down, and the old man came out to put on another.

"Please, is it a long way to Elmwood Road?" said Dickie.

His voice sounded funny because he had been crying so much.

"No, not so far," said the old man. "Why do you want to go there?"

"I live there," said Dickie.

"Well, well, you go straight down the street that way till you come to the main road, and then a penny bus will take you to Elmwood Road. Have you got a penny?"

"No."

The old man fumbled in a till and took out a penny.

"Now run off home," he said. "Time you were in bed. You'll get your death in this rain."

Dickie took the penny, and began to run along the street. It was still raining. The clock struck seven as he ran.

Joy stood at the window. It was just like one of those nightmares in which you tell yourself that it can't possibly be true, that it must be a dream. Only she knew that this wasn't a dream. Dickie was somewhere out in the cold and rain, frightened, unhappy, perhaps even now——; no, she'd go mad if she let herself think of that.

Her anxiety had grown heavier and heavier during tea as the minutes went by, and still Dickie did not come home. She had tried not to show it, to be cheerful and ordinary, not to frighten the children. Miss Nash had, as usual, been ready with futile reassurances, "I expect they've kept him back to tidy his desk." "Perhaps he's gone home to tea with one of the other boys." ... And all the time that sick, dragging feeling like an iron weight in her stomach told her that something must have happened to him. Horribly clear pictures came to her of Dickie lying in the road, his eyes closed, his bright head in the mud.

Then—the culmination of the horror—came that hateful policeman with his, "A real, bad boy, breaking windows, and giving false names and addresses." She had flared out at him angrily, and sent him away abashed and crestfallen, but there had been stark terror behind her anger. She saw Dickie in the police court, heard the policeman giving his monstrous evidence ("A real, bad boy, breaking windows, and giving false names and addresses"), heard the magistrate say, "Reformatory" . . . saw Dickie taken from her.

Miss Nash, of course, was unbearably sympathetic, making her cups of tea that she didn't want, bringing her aspirins, shaking up the cushions of her chair as if she were an invalid, quoting pieces of bright helpful poetry. Joy was glad, in a way, of the exasperation that Miss Nash made her feel. It was a counter irritant to her anxiety. She knew that Bruce was busy at the office, and for a long time she could not bring herself to ring him up. When she did so, she was told that he had just set out for home.

And then at twenty past seven came a knock that could only be Dickie's. Joy rushed to the door. It was such a sodden, bedraggled, little figure, his face swollen and streaked with dirt and tears, that just for a second she didn't recognise him. Then they fell into each other's arms, both weeping unrestrainedly.

She would not let him talk at all till she had given him a hot bath, and a basin of bread and milk in bed. Then she let him tell her all about it, her arm about him.

"And what made you come home in the end, darling?" she said.

He was just going to say, "Gran told me to," but stopped. Gran was dead, of course, so she couldn't have told him to. It would have been a silly thing to say.

"I don't know," he said.

Bruce was there when she came down, sitting in the arm-chair by the fireplace, wearily relaxed. His plain face, with its ugly misshapen mouth, looked grey with fatigue. Joy's eyes deepened with pity as they rested on him.

"Have you had a bad day, darling?" she said.

He roused himself and smiled at her.

"No, quite good," he said.

She sank on to the hearth-rug at his feet and told him about

Dickie. "He's been punished quite enough, dear," she ended. "If I were you, I shouldn't even speak to him about it."

He took her hand, kissed it, then laid its soft coolness against his throbbing head.

"Very well," he said.

He had had to bear the full brunt of his employer's nerve-wracked irritability all day, and he didn't want to do anything in the world now, but just rest like this near Joy.

Chapter Eighteen

"You've spoken to her?"

"Yes, she won't divorce me."

Olivia was sitting forward in her arm-chair, her hands clasped, her eyes fixed on the fire. Stephen stood on the hearth-rug, looking down at her.

"Why not?"

"Sheer devilry. She doesn't love me, but she doesn't want to let me go if she can help it. . . . She'd obviously be glad to be without me in lots of ways. She wants to live at an hotel. I've never understood her. . . . It makes no difference, of course."

"You mean——?"

"We must just go away."

"Yes. . . . I see."

Both were silent; then she spoke with an effort, her eyes still fixed on the fire.

"We've got to talk this out, Stephen."

"We've talked it out. We've decided what we're going to do."

"I think we have when I'm with you. Then you go away, and I'm not sure. I lie awake all night, thinking about it. You see I want you so dreadfully, I think it would kill me to have to give you up now. But—there's your career, and——"

She stopped.

"Yes?" he said. "And what——"

She hesitated, and then said, "Nothing else. Just your career."

"I've told you that my career's nothing to me. It's you I want. My dear, have you such a poor opinion of me that you think I'm incapable of supporting you?"

"Don't, Stephen," she said sharply. "You know it isn't that. Very well, I won't worry about that any longer."

"You should be glad, as I am, to risk something for our love."

"Yes," she agreed humbly. "I'll look on it like that. I'm sorry, darling, It was for your sake, not my own that—I felt——"

"I know, my sweet. But you mustn't."

"I'd hate you to have to suffer because of me. It was only that, Stephen."

"I know. I know. . . . But you've promised me not to think of that again. How are things going with Derek?"

She threw out her hands in a gesture of weary helplessness.

"He's in a very bad state of nerves," she said, "and I'm the obvious outlet, I suppose."

Derek's temper was growing steadily worse. Whatever she did, nowadays, was wrong. If she prepared an appetizing meal for him in the evening, he stormed at her for extravagance, if she prepared a plain one, he stormed at her as an incompetent housekeeper. When he wasn't storming at her, he was wrapped in a heavy scowling surliness. Often he refused to answer when she spoke to him.

"The remedy's simple," said Stephen. "Why should we wait?"

"I've told you, Stephen. I can't leave him just now. If his business recovers I can leave him without a qualm, and if it goes smash he'll be glad to be rid of the responsibility of me. But just now—I told you before—my leaving him on the top of everything else might be the last straw to him."

"How is his business?"

"I don't know. He won't speak of it. He gets furious if I mention it, but I conclude that it's in a pretty bad way. He's no ready money at all, and we're rather badly in debt to the trades people."

He frowned.

"I want to get you away from it all."

"Be patient, darling," she pleaded. "We shall soon have left it all behind us. This will be like a bad dream to me, and Wanda will be like a bad dream to you."

"Yes."

He spoke absently. His eyes looked through her, beyond her.

"What are you thinking of, Stephen?"

His eyes focussed her again quickly.

"Nothing."

"Are you thinking of Clarissa?"

He flushed.

"No."

She smiled—a rather twisted smile.

"You're a poor liar, Stephen. You were thinking of Clarissa, weren't you?"

"The thought of her had come into my mind for a second," he admitted.

"Why shouldn't we have her with us?" she said, slowly. "I'd love to."

"Wanda wouldn't let her go."

"How do you know?"

"I've asked her."

Something faintly jarring had crept into the atmosphere.

"Stephen," she said, slowly, "why didn't you tell me that you'd asked Wanda about Clarissa?"

"What was there to tell? She said, 'no,' so things were as they had been."

"I see. . . . You'll miss Clarissa, won't you?"

His eyes slid away from her as he answered carelessly, "My dear, she's only a child. I was very lonely, and she's been a wonderful little companion. When I've got you. . . . It's very sweet of you to suggest having Clarissa."

"It was rather a belated suggestion, evidently."

Then she bit her lip. But he had not noticed the faint irony of her tone. His thoughts were elsewhere.

"I'll talk to Wanda again," he said. "She cares nothing for the child. It was merely spitefulness."

"You must try to make her understand how much Clarissa means to you, how terribly you'll miss her."

"Yes," he agreed absently. Then he looked at her in surprise. "What's the matter, Olivia?"

Her eyes were bright with tears.

"Nothing," she whispered, turning her head away. "It's just nerves, I suppose."

He was on his knees by her chair.

"My precious, my darling. It's a hateful time for you. It will soon be over. Just look ahead. Think of the time when we'll have each other always. My sweet, I love you so. ... I love you so."

He stroked back her hair, kissing her on the eyes and forehead. She drew away from him, smiling unsteadily.

"Stephen, you're a wonderful father. You ought to have had dozens of children."

"You won't worry about anything any more?"

"No."

"You'll just think of the time when we shall have each other."

"Yes. ... You'd better go now, Stephen."

"Why?"

"I think I'd like to be alone."

"You've promised?"

"Yes."

He kissed her, and went.

Though she had wanted to be alone, solitude brought her no comfort.

The heaviness that pressed upon her spirit frightened her. It was like falling down into a black, bottomless pit. ... She tried to face what it was that was forcing her down into the abyss, then sheered away quickly. ... She must fill her mind with something else. She went to the piano and began to play *Au Clair de la Lune*. That made it worse. Before she fell in love with Stephen, she had been learning Italian. She had not touched it since. She took the book from her shelves, and, sitting down at her bureau, began to write an exercise. She was doing this when the maid announced Christopher.

"You're busy," he said. "Perhaps you'd rather I didn't interrupt."

The gentleness of his manner touched her. She put out her hand to him.

"Stay, Patrino," she said. "I'd like you to stay."

She had begun to call him Patrino a few years ago. "Father" seemed too familiar, and "Mr. Mainwaring" too formal. For some obscure reason it infuriated Rachel to hear her use the name.

He looked over her shoulder at the book.

"I didn't know you were studying Italian," he said.

"It's rather spasmodic studying. I began it months ago. I suddenly realised how ignorant I was, and that I must do something about it. It really makes no difference. When I've got to the end of all these books I shall be just as ignorant as I was before. One's ignorance simply doesn't bear thinking of, does it?"

He had sat down on the chesterfield near her.

"Don't think of it," he smiled. "Think of what the thrush said."

"What did the thrush say?"

"Don't you know?

"Oh, fret not after knowledge—I have none,
And yet my song comes native with the warmth,
Oh, fret not after knowledge—I have none,
And yet the evening listens."

"That's rather nice," she said slowly. "Whose is it?"

"Keats."

"Say it again so that I can remember it."

He repeated it. She listened dreamily to the gentle, cultured voice.

"They taught you how to speak properly when you were young, didn't they?" she said. "They had time for things like that then, I suppose."

He stood up and looked at the book-shelves above her bureau.

"You read a lot."

"Yes," she said. "I read, and play the piano. It's what's mistakenly called having resources in oneself. It's so foolish, isn't it? No one has resources in himself. Put anyone in a room with nothing at all to do, and he'll go mad in a week. A book is no more a resource in oneself than a cinema or a night club."

He smiled.

"I suppose not. . . ."

In the silence that followed she was acutely conscious of the understanding that had always been between them.

"Isn't it funny, Patrino," she said, slowly, "that life gives you no peace? From the minute you can remember anything, you're pulled this way and that."

"Sanity, my dear," he said, "is a balance of opposite forces, but there must be opposite forces. There must be tension, some element of strain or difficulty. If you eliminate that, you create boredom, and boredom is insanity."

He was talking mechanically, wondering how to approach the object of his visit. He would not try to approach it in a roundabout way, as he had done with Joy. He would blurt it out, tell her the whole story. She moved at her desk so that the light fell upon her face, and he saw suddenly the desperate unhappiness of her eyes.

He put his hand on her shoulder.

"What's the matter, my child?"

She turned her head away and took his hand, holding it to her cheek.

"Is it Derek?" he said.

"Partly."

"What is it? Tell me, my dear. I'm an old man. Perhaps I can understand. Don't you love him any more?"

She spoke in a quick, unsteady voice, her head still turned away from him.

"No. . . . I'm frightened, Patrino. It's so hard to see one's way. I'm sorry for Derek. I'm not the sort of wife he should have had. He should have had someone stupid and adoring. I suppose that when I married him I was stupid and adoring, and he can't see why I should have changed. I'd have gone through hell for him then, because he had a nice smile and a straight nose, and he can't understand why I should ever have stopped feeling like that. Being in love's a sort of madness."

"I understand, my dear," he said quietly.

"You don't, Patrino. You and Derek's mother were happy. You loved no one but each other. You're a darling, but—you can't quite understand."

Subconsciously he thought: She doesn't know. It's no use asking her.

"It isn't as if we had children," she was saying.

He looked at the tightened corners of her lips, the bright unhappiness of her eyes, and knew what she was trying to tell him.

"There's someone else," he said gently.

"Yes. I'm going to leave Derek, and go away with him. Do you think I'm wicked?"

"I could never think that, my dear. I shall pray always for your happiness."

"Patrino, supposing I hadn't made up my mind to do that, and I'd asked your advice, what would you have said?"

"I'd have said that no one in the world but yourself can decide."

She was silent for some moments, then said abruptly: "It's Stephen Arnold. You might as well know."

He said nothing. Somehow he wished it had not been Stephen Arnold. There was not a better or kinder man than Stephen Arnold in the world, and yet there was a strain of weakness in him that Christopher recognised, because it was in himself as well. To him, as to Christopher, it was always easiest to take the way of least resistance. He had seen Stephen frequently lately. Christopher had begun to take a "constitutional" over Heston Common on Sunday afternoon, and he generally met Stephen Arnold and his little girl there. The sight of them always interested him. They seemed more like a pair of lovers than father and daughter, the child hanging on to his arm, her face upraised to his, his bent to her. He thought of Stephen's wife, with her hard, bright, tinkling worldliness. It had been a tragic marriage. So, probably, had been Derek's and Olivia's. ... He sighed deeply.

"What will happen to the child?" he said.

"She'll stay with her mother, of course," said Olivia casually.

The confidence between them was suddenly and mysteriously shattered. He felt that she wanted to be rid of him. He rose uncertainly.

"You'll let me know if I can help you?" he said.

She took his hand again and raised it to her lips impulsively.

"I'm sorry to bring this trouble to you, Patrino," she said.

When he had gone, she sat staring in front of her. It would all be so simple if it were not for Wanda. She and Stephen and Clarissa. He would not miss children if he had Clarissa. She loved Clarissa, too. It would be in every way as if she were their own child. . . . Everything would be straightforward if it were not for Wanda. . . . She imagined someone's ringing her up and saying, "Have you heard about Wanda Arnold? She died quite suddenly last night."

She shivered, and, starting from her seat, began to pace to and fro in the room.

Suddenly she stopped. The eyes of Susan's photograph on the mantelpiece (a photograph of the oil-painting that hung in the drawing-room at Christopher's) seemed to be following her. . . . She went up to it and looked at it searchingly.

"You understand," she said aloud. "You always understood. Tell me what to do."

But the eyes only smiled at her, tender, faintly amused.

Christopher walked away from the house, feeling anxious and unhappy. He loved Olivia, and things were going wrong with her—more wrong than she had let him see. He had been conscious all the time of a deeper unhappiness in her than she had shown him. She had been desperate, not knowing where to turn. She had only let him touch the skirt of her trouble. He was an old man . . . clumsy, rather stupid. She could not have confided in him, of course. A woman needed a woman to help her. He turned suddenly, and began to walk in the direction of Joy's house.

Joy opened the door to him herself. She looked flushed and a little untidy. It was washing day, and she was helping to iron the clothes in the kitchen, working very hard so as to get it done before Miss Nash came home with the children. She felt a wave of irritation with him, as she held open the door for him to enter. Surely he might have known that Monday was washing-day, and that she would be busy. Of course, that was the worst of men who had retired. They had such a lot of time on their hands. It had been different when Mother was alive. He had gone everywhere with her. But now—she hoped he wasn't going to get into the habit of dropping in like this at odd moments. She really had not the time for it. The Saturday gatherings ought to be enough. Those and the times they asked him to tea, and made preparations, and expected him. She did not want to be inhospitable, but, with four children, every second of the day had to be mapped out in order to get through the work. He ought to have understood that. . . . After all, a man need never be lonely. There were golf, bridge, clubs. He ought to go for another motor tour. She hoped that he was not going to talk as he had talked when he called last week, meandering on, and on, about things they had all forgotten long ago.

She hid every trace of her irritation as she took him into the drawing-room, and lit the gas fire. The dining-room was the family sitting-room and nursery combined, and there was always a good coal fire in it, but at present she was taking advantage of the children's absence to dry some woollens there. A laden clothes-horse stood round the fire, and the air was damp and steamy.

"And are you feeling better, Father?" she began, cheerfully. "You're looking much better."

"Oh, I'm very well."

"I think you ought to go away on another little motor tour. You enjoyed the other one, didn't you?"

"Yes."

"And what about golf? You were going to take that up, weren't you? Have you begun it yet?"

He looked at her with a faint smile, as if he saw into her mind.

"No, but I manage to fill up my time very well. I'm fond of walking, you know, and Lethbridge often comes in the evening, and we have a game of two-handed bridge."

She glanced at the clock. Miss Nash and the children would be back in about ten minutes' time, and, if she had not got the ironing finished, there would be no time to do it till the children were in bed.

"Joy," he said, suddenly. "Olivia's very unhappy."

She shot him a bright glance of fear.

"I can't do anything," she said breathlessly.

She felt a sudden wave of anger with him. It was cruel of him to say that, to make demands on her to which she could not possibly respond. To expect her, with all her heart full to overflowing of her own daily anxieties, to have thought for Olivia, Olivia who was hard, and sophisticated, and self-sufficient, and superbly able to take care of herself.

"I can't do anything," she said again, terrified that he was going to destroy that picture of an Olivia, who was hard, and sophisticated, and self-sufficient. He said nothing more, however, only began to ask after the children, as if nothing had been said about Olivia, and soon rose to take his leave.

When he had gone, Joy went back to the kitchen and went on with the ironing. She did it vehemently, with many unnecessary bangs and pats. ... It was wrong to interfere in other people's affairs. Father ought not to have asked her to. She had been quite right to refuse. She could not possibly have done anything else. Yet, though she finished the ironing before the children came in, and though the woollens dried beautifully, and Dickie had got full marks for his arithmetic, and Bobs said, "Boy on bicycle," quite distinctly, she felt unaccountably depressed all the evening.

Chapter Nineteen

DEREK and Olivia gave their annual bridge drive as usual at the end of October.

Olivia had suggested to Derek that they should not give it this year, but he had turned on her with an angry, "Why not?"

"You know we're not well off just now," she had said quietly.

His face had darkened.

"Who says we're not well off just now?"

She shrugged faintly. "You're always saying so."

He denied it hotly.

"And what do you suppose people would think if we didn't give it?"

"Probably that we're very sensible."

"My position in this town, of course, means nothing to you."

"Derek, don't be childish. Not giving a party won't affect your position in this town. Every business has its bad times. People would understand."

That was the worst thing she could have said. It was as if she had smote the Image in the face. He flew into one of his blind rages.

After that she went forward with her preparations, ordering everything on the same scale as in previous years.

The trades people's manner to her had changed lately. Their accounts remained unpaid, and they were beginning to suspect the soundness of Derek's position. Derek himself waved their books aside impatiently, when Olivia, steeled for another outburst, drew his attention to them.

"There's no hurry at all. My dear girl, you know nothing whatever of business methods. Those people like their accounts to run on. . . . "

They have a curious way of showing it, she thought, remembering the curtness of their manner, but she said nothing further to Derek.

Ordinarily she would have found the position unbearably humiliating, but her life in Ravenham seemed now only a dream to her. Her real life would begin when she left Ravenham with Stephen.

She wished that she had not gone to Wanda's party last week. She had not wanted to go, and at first had decided to refuse the invitation. Then she had begun to think of it as a challenge that it would be cowardly to refuse. So she had gone.

Stephen had been in the hall when she arrived, and he had started towards her, eagerly, but a parlourmaid, coming downstairs, had said to him, "Please, sir, Miss Clarissa asked me to remind you about saying good night to her."

He had said, "Oh, yes, I had not forgotten," and gone upstairs two steps at a time. Wanda had laughed, and said in her hard, bright voice, "He's quite crazy about the child."

A maid had taken Olivia up to Wanda's bedroom, and on the way they had passed a room whose door was ajar. She had glanced in, and had seen Stephen's figure reflected in a mirror on the wall. He was bending over Clarissa's bed, and Clarissa's arms were clasped tightly about his neck.

There was a photograph of Clarissa in a silver frame on the mantelpiece of the drawing-room, where they played bridge. To Olivia the childish face, with its innocent eyes and sensitive drooping lips, seemed to dominate the room. That, and Wanda, smart, and hard, and brilliant; Wanda with the thin, reddened lips that were cruel and amused. If only Clarissa had been Wanda's child, not Stephen's, if her lips had not had that sensitive droop, her eyes that wondering innocence. . . . It was impossible to see the two of them together without wanting to protect her against Wanda.

Wanda's party had increased her shrinking from her own. When her guests were finally assembled in the drawing-room, a vivacious, chattering crowd, she felt so far away from them as to be in a different world. She imagined them chattering like this in a month's time, eagerly, vivaciously, over her elopement with Stephen, exchanging confidences ("My dear, it's probably been going on for *years*"). . . . Well, it wouldn't affect her and Stephen, they would be far enough away. They would go to Fontainebleau first, Stephen had said. They could live there cheaply, and he loved the forest. She had not been there since she was a schoolgirl. She remembered a long, green glade, and at the end of it a stag standing motionless, alert, his antlers held high. She saw herself and Stephen wandering through the forest . . . but the picture was dim, and blurred, and unreal. It faded away, and—vividly, vividly real—came the picture of Stephen leaning over a child's bed, two small thin arms clasped tightly round his neck. . . .

Derek, as always under the stimulus of playing host, was growing noisy—boasting, making futile jokes, patronising people, parading the Image.

"We've got fond of this little house, but there's hardly room to move in it. We're really going to move out of it next year. I'd like a place with some shooting."

She thought: Probably everyone in the room knows that we can't pay the tradesmen's bills. He's like an ostrich digging his head into the sand. . . . She was ashamed that Stephen, who was so quiet, and unassuming, and sincere, should see Derek like this. She felt as if he must be wondering distrustfully whether there were something in her that he had not yet met, that had made her choose a man like Derek for her husband. She wanted to say: "He must have been like this, of course, but somehow I didn't see him like this."

She could endure Derek's parading the Image, because she was used to it, but what she felt she could not endure before Stephen, what she prayed she would not have to endure, was his making her take a part in the puppet show as the Image's wife. He did that sometimes. He would throw an arm round her shoulder affectionately, call her "darling", and tease her with a tender playfulness that he only showed before a room full of people. He was not consciously playing the hypocrite. He saw her on such occasions, not as she was, but as the wife of the Image, blindly adoring, docile, amenable, the "dear little woman" he had mistakenly thought her when he married her.

Christopher (who had arrived with Lethbridge among the earliest guests) sat at a table in a corner of the room watching Olivia. He saw the light shine in her eyes, the glow kindle in her cheeks, when Stephen Arnold, tall and stooping, arrived with his sparkling little wife. His eyes went to Stephen, searching his face as if for reassurance. Then he sighed as if he had not found it. There are some people who can defy the world's conventions without suffering, but Stephen was not one of them. His conscience was too tender. However much he loved Olivia, he would never be sure that he had done right in taking her out of the protected area. He would suffer acutely in the slights that the world would be prompt to offer her. For Wanda would never divorce him. It would give her a keenly malicious pleasure to refuse him his freedom. A strong man would have taken Olivia away at once. He would not have agreed to this futile plan of waiting.

Olivia was still receiving the guests. Her sudden glow had faded, and she looked white and tired. Stephen, sitting at a table with his wife, was watching her. Christopher wanted to cry out to him. "Don't look at her like that, you fool. Everyone will know." Then he saw that Wanda's sharp eyes were fixed on her husband. They moved from him to Olivia, and her lips curled into a smile. . . .

Joy and Bruce had arrived. Joy looked very matronly and preoccupied. She kissed Christopher, and said, "How are you, Father, dear?" but he knew that she was not really there. She was at home with Dickie and Billy and Laura and Bobs. Bruce looked fagged. Dawes was a beast, and enjoyed bullying the poor, little man, thought Christopher, but Bruce was wise to endure it. He wouldn't get another job easily if he gave up this one, and he was happy enough in his home life. One couldn't have everything. His weariness always accentuated his ugliness, and Christopher, looking at him, wondered for the thousandth time what had made Joy fall in love with him. He had prophesied that her love would not survive ten days' marriage, and it had survived more than ten years. Probably she would have quarrelled in less than a month with the handsome, young spark he had imagined as her husband. Nature had odd ways of doing things, but presumably knew what she was about.

Frank and Rachel arrived last of all. Frank looked rather worried, as usual. The mischievous schoolboy was still there, but buried a little more deeply every time Christopher saw him. He would soon have disappeared altogether. He showed now only in a sudden smile, an occasional tone of voice. They shook hands affectionately. Christopher felt nearer to Frank than to either of the other two. The other two had no need of him, and Frank had a need—inarticulate, almost unconscious, but still a need. He felt that he and Frank would draw nearer to each other as the years went on.

Rachel had gone to a table in a corner of the room. He could not see her because Lethbridge stood in the way, but he could imagine her sitting there, tense and outraged, because no one was taking any notice of her. Probably before the end of the evening she would consider herself deliberately insulted by everyone in the room. And the worst of it was that you could not help feeling sorry for her, though you felt sorrier still for Frank.

Lethbridge moved away, and he got a clear view of her. She was sitting gazing dreamily in front of her, a far-away smile on her lips, unaware of anything going on around her. He had never seen her look like that before. Nor had he ever seen her so beautiful. There was a soft glow about her. She looked like a young girl. Surely *she* wasn't falling in love with someone. . . .

People were taking their places for the first game. Derek's voice was raised above the subsiding murmur of conversation.

"I'd had no business training at all, but, when I took over this do, I cut out all unnecessary work in a week and literally halved it. Merely a question of common sense and ordinary intelligence." A rather foolish-looking girl, who was standing near him, said:

"Ah, but everyone hasn't got your brains, you know."

Derek smiled delightedly.

Stephen passed Olivia on their way to the tables.

"Let it be soon, my dear," he whispered, "I can't bear this much longer."

At the sound of his voice all her doubts and fears faded away. He loved her as she loved him, unalterably, eternally. Their way lay straight and clear before them. Nothing could hinder them.

She played first with Mrs. Dunton, and they finished their game early. Almost before they had finished, Mrs. Dunton (whose blackened lashes, coated with powder, gave her face a slightly sinister aspect) began her mechanical depreciation of all their common acquaintances. Mrs. Dunton was not an ill-natured woman, but her half-unconscious knowledge of her own limitations made an unceasing calumniation of other people necessary to her self-esteem.

Olivia made mechanical comments, but heard nothing that she said.

You could live very cheaply abroad. Stephen could write. He had had one or two articles accepted already by a good review. Some years ago he had written a play. He had not tried to place it. He could take it away and revise it. If that were not successful he could try another. He had ideas and a feeling for style. He had had no incentive to work till now. . . . She saw them in a tiny villa overlooking the Mediterranean—roses, and olives, and vines. . . . Stephen writing in the little loggia. Or—he had a flair for antiques. They might set up a small antique business. She could help him in that.

She moved on to the next table, where Wanda was waiting for her. All her newly-found serenity left her as she sat down opposite Wanda. The bright, malicious eyes, and the mocking, cynical curve of the red lips were like fingers of ice on her heart. And the malice of the smile seemed to be especially for her. The game finished, and the other two moved on. She and Wanda were left alone at the table.

"How charming everything looks," said Wanda, hardly troubling to put even a pretence of sincerity into her voice. "And everyone turned up in time, too, so that we could begin promptly. I was afraid that Stephen and I were going to be late."

"Were you?"

Olivia was looking round the room, as if she scarcely saw or heard Wanda, but she was so acutely aware of her that she was clenching hands and teeth in her effort to appear unconscious.

Wanda went on in her hard, metallic voice.

"He had to go and say good night to Clarissa, of course, at the last minute, and I thought the child was never going to let him go. They have a lot of ridiculous imaginary people, you know, and they make up absurd imaginary adventures for them."

Olivia said nothing.

Wanda looked at her till she had to turn and meet her eyes. There was a few moments' silence. Then Wanda spoke slowly and meaningly, the red lips curved in malicious triumph.

"He'd never be happy without Clarissa, you know. He may think he would, but he'd soon find out his mistake."

The blood faded from Olivia's cheeks and lips, her pulses beat deafeningly in her ears. Wanda knew . . .

Frank looked at her from across the room, and spoke to Derek, who was at the same table.

"Olivia looks as if she was going to faint, old man. This room's too hot, you know."

And then came the culmination of the nightmare—Derek bending over her, playing the affectionate, solicitous husband ("What is it, darling? Aren't you well?")—while Wanda still watched her, smiling.

She sat up, tense and quivering, digging her teeth into her lip, and the blood flamed into her cheeks again.

"I'm all right," she protested, unsteadily. "Quite all right. It was nothing."

"She only wanted someone to make a fuss over her," laughed Derek, with the playful tenderness that belonged to the Image-husband.

Someone opened a window, and the excitement died away.

Christopher stood with Lethbridge and a group of other men round the fire in the dining-room after supper. The women had gone back to the drawing-room, where they were engaged chiefly in repairing their make-up. The Vicar was becoming rather prosy, as he always did when people listened to him. Someone said that heroism had died out since the war, and he was holding forth in his pulpit manner, saying that the average father of the average middle-class family was a greater hero than any V.C. in the war.

"When one thinks of the load of responsibilities he carries, the constant sacrifices demanded of him, the fear of illness and unemployment that hangs over him continually——."

It was quite a good point, but he was obviously going to labour it till he became a nuisance.

Ronald Handley, whose rooms overlooked Whitehall, was inviting young Marvel to come up to see the next Opening of Parliament procession.

"It really is a wonderful little pageant," he was saying. "It's typical of England."

"Pageant isn't typical of England," said old Templeton, who had been manager of Barclay's Bank in High Street for the last twenty years. "I'll tell you what's typical of England. I saw it in the last year of the war. I saw a puny, undersized, little Cockney Tommy coaxing a half-starved mongrel to him at a street corner to stroke it and give it part of the sandwich he was eating. I said, 'That's England', and it's meant England to me ever since."

"Kindness to animals, certainly, is the greatest characteristic of England," put in Beardman, the parish church senior curate, in his ultra Oxford accents.

Lethbridge turned on him savagely.

"It isn't and it never has been. Of English men perhaps. But not of English women. There has never been a greater piece of hypocrisy than the English woman's attitude to animals. Watch them swarming into anti-vivisectionist meetings, wearing the furs of animals that have died in far greater agony than any vivisectionist ever inflicts. I met an old trapper once, who'd given up the work because its cruelty made him sick. I shouldn't like to repeat to you the tales he told me. ... And I shouldn't like to repeat to you his opinion of the women who make the work necessary. In the last trap he visited he found a bear with its teeth broken from trying to sever the steel trap, the paw that was caught in the trap gangrened and stinking, the rest of its body torn by its own agonised biting. Heaven knows how long it had been there. It was still alive. That wasn't by any means the worst sight he'd seen—he'd seen seals skinned alive because it's easier than doing it when they're dead—but it was after that he decided that he'd rather starve than visit another trap. So that when a woman, wearing furs that have meant the hellish torture of an animal (and very few don't), protests to me against vivisection, or tells me, with tears in her eyes, about the stomach-ache of her pet dog, you can imagine I don't waste much sympathy on her."

"They don't know the facts," put in young Boardman, rather shocked by Lethbridge's vehemence.

"They don't want to know them," muttered Lethbridge. "The facts are there—open to everyone."

"But there's a law, surely, isn't there, that the traps have to be visited at certain, short intervals," said Handley.

"It's a law that's never kept," said Lethbridge. "Weather conditions make it an impossibility. . . . I don't blame the trappers, God knows. I blame the tender-hearted Christian women of England and other countries who demand such horrors. If they could have watched the deaths of the creatures whose skins they wear so elegantly, they would be haunted for the rest of their lives."

He subsided, growling, and there was a constrained silence. It was generally felt that Lethbridge had rather exceeded good manners in his vehemence. Derek rose with his charming smile.

"Well, we all know what women are," he said, indulgently. "Shall we go in for the next game?"

The guests dawdled and gossiped in groups when the party was over, and finally set off homewards, congratulating Olivia on the success of the evening.

Wanda took leave of her with a slow, secret smile.

"You don't look well, my dear," she said, with mock solicitude. "Why don't you get Derek to take you away for a nice, long holiday—a second honeymoon?"

From half-way down the steps she called back, "Take care of her, Derek," and laughed, as she disappeared into the darkness.

Olivia's cheeks were ashen, her bright eyes hunted and desperate.

When the door had closed on their last guest, she turned to her husband.

"I'll go straight upstairs to bed if you don't mind, Derek. I'm frightfully tired. Good night."

Derek stood in the hall watching her in scowling silence till she vanished round the bend of the stairs, then went back into the drawing-room. It wore a dreary after-the-party air, chairs and tables pushed awry, ash-trays full of cigarette ends and bonbon papers, the atmosphere heavy with smoke. Someone's scarf still lay over a chair, and there was a silk embroidered bag on one of the tables. He wandered into the dining-room. The remains of supper made that room even more desolate than the other. He returned to the drawing-room. Just like Olivia to have gone to bed like this and left him without a word. His high spirits had continued till the last guest had gone, but at every step he took in the deserted rooms they sank lower. Terror closed over him when he tried to face what lay ahead of him. He didn't see how he could hold out much longer. Creditors were pressing him, and, what was worse, were beginning to realise how things stood with him. He was dismissing workers daily because he had no money for them, and nothing for them to do. His affairs were chaotic. He did not know, and dared not find out, exactly how much he owed. When he thought of public failure . . . people watching him, whispering about him in the streets of Ravenham ("He's failed, you know") . . . this house that he had affected to despise being sold . . . the Image publicly hurled from its pedestal amid laughter and mockery . . . the sweat broke out all over his body, his heart quickened, and his breath came and went unevenly.

He need not survive the Image, of course. There was a way out. The idea of suicide had always appealed to him. There was something dramatic, something almost dignified about it. Better than standing before the world naked, stripped of all his glory. But, whenever he seriously considered it, he remembered his mother, and knew that he could never take that way. His mother. . . . Things had gone wrong with him ever since she died. Even his failure would not have been so terrifying if he had had the knowledge of her love sustaining him. Her actual death had affected him little. He had not been conscious of any deep bond between them. It was not till now—when he actively needed her love, and turned to it instinctively to find it gone—that he knew what it had meant to him. Her love for him, her first-born, had been different in quality from the love she bore the others. It had been stronger, more primitive, more deeply rooted. Without his knowledge, it had formed the background of his life. Whatever he was, whatever he did, it would never fail him.

He realised her death for the first time. Panic swept over him, and he felt like a little boy left alone in the dark, like a tight-rope walker when the safety net beneath him is suddenly withdrawn. Stark fear had lain behind his bravado all evening. Olivia? Her love had been a different sort of love from his mother's. It had been composed of passion and admiration, and it had failed him. She had withdrawn herself from him. The loss of her love, of which he was half-unconsciously aware, humiliated him in his own eyes, and made him fiercely resentful against her, as if she were responsible for everything that had gone wrong with him. He threw his scowling gaze around the room. What must this party have cost? He deliberately forgot that he had insisted on giving it, and set it as another grudge against her in his mind. It was her extravagance that was ruining him. . . .

Chapter Twenty

IT was the day of Barbara's birthday party. Her guests were to be Dickie, Billy, Laura, Bobs, Clarissa Arnold, Cicely Rainham, some of the Melliners, and a few school friends. The Rainhams lived at the end of the road. Relations between Rachel and Mrs. Rainham had been rather strained lately, owing to Mrs. Rainham's habit of borrowing such household articles as tin-openers and egg-beaters, and omitting to return them, but last week Cicely, having heard rumours of Barbara's party, had invited Barbara to tea, and so Cicely had been included in Barbara's party as an eleventh-hour guest. The Melliners were the large and noisy family of the Rector of Ravenham. They divided themselves into two gangs, each of which tried to score off the other by tricks and practical jokes. One of them belonged to neither side, but was an umpire who kept the score solemnly in an exercise book. People giving children's parties in Ravenham always asked "some of the Melliners." The Melliners *en masse* would have wrecked any party.

Rachel took the matter of Barbara's birthday-party very seriously. Each guest appeared to her in the light of an emissary sent by its family to spy out the nakedness of her land. She felt that, should her silver not be spotless, should her cakes not be light as feathers, should her jellies not be as shapely as their moulds, should there be a speck of dust showing in hall, dining-room, or drawing-room, the whole of Ravenham would be laughing at her to-morrow.

In order to have no weak spot in her armour, she got up before daybreak and set to work cleaning down the house. None of the rooms needed cleaning, but she wanted to be on the safe side. By lunch time she was utterly exhausted, and her temper worn to shreds. She scolded the children continually. Barbara cried whenever she was scolded, partly from habit, and partly because it was the quickest way of stopping the scolding, but, in spite of it all, she was pleased and excited at the thought of being the heroine of the day. She was very glad to be nine, too, because it was a step nearer ten, and she had decided many years ago that ten was her favourite age. She tried to behave like a grown-up person at breakfast, saying:

"I saw Mrs. Belton in the town yesterday and I thought she was very funny with me."

"Funny with me," was one of Rachel's phrases. Frank lowered his paper to tell her sharply not to talk nonsense, but Rachel was sombrely interested. How was she funny?

"Just smiled at me quickly and then went on," said Barbara.

She felt delightfully grown-up as she said it.

Jonathan was under a cloud. He had fallen in with his gang of "common" boys after school yesterday, and they had pursued a rival gang through the darkening street. A heady excitement, an intoxicating lust of adventure, had seized Jonathan. A desperate hand-to-hand struggle had taken place, which was ended only by the arrival of a policeman. The pursuit had begun again, the pursuing band headed by a battered, torn, wildly exultant Jonathan. He was all the heroes in all the world who had ever led their armies to battle. His war-cry rang out shrilly to the heavens. Seeing his quarry running down the front of a block of houses and round to the back, he plunged through a garden to intercept them, still uttering his battle-cry. He was caught by the enraged householder, recognised, and taken home ignominiously. The band escaped. The householder happened to be a patient of Frank's ("He would be," said Frank bitterly), and gave Frank lengthy advice on not letting his children run wild in the streets. Frank had shown quite plainly that he did not relish the advice, and, when his visitor departed, there was an unspoken understanding between them that the next time he wanted a doctor he would call in someone else.

Frank had put into the punishment of Jonathan a good deal of the annoyance that he felt with his ex-patient. Jonathan felt resentful and bewildered. His adventure had been, in his eyes, a heroic exploit, an epic. With such feelings as his, the medieval nobles had led their followers to battle in the streets of Florence. And it was a crime. It was "disgracing his parents". It wasn't "behaving like a gentleman".

"I don't care," he thought defiantly, as he lay in bed, and thought over the evening's events. "I don't care. I like fighting, and I don't care if it is wicked."

Then he slid into a dream, in which he and his band pursued the householder up and down the streets of Ravenham.

His clothes, of course, were in a disgraceful state, and he had a black eye the next morning, so that Rachel joined her displeasure to Frank's ("What ever will people *think*?"), and Barbara, who did not want to hazard her birthday position by siding with the criminal against justice, also ignored him.

Jonathan had to go to school as usual in the afternoon, but Barbara was allowed to stay at home to help Rachel prepare for the party. She felt very important, but the actual pleasure of the proceeding was negligible, as Rachel was now so over-tired and nervy, that she snapped at her continually. The climax came when Barbara, who had set the table alone, and expected praise and admiration, received, instead, a scolding for putting the cups on the right hand of the tea-table instead of the left. Then she sobbed in real earnest. ("It's my birthday, and you're being so horrid to me"), and Rachel, filled with sudden remorse, dropped on to the floor and hugged her, and began to sob too. They comforted each other, and were both in an overwrought state of nerves by the time the guests began to arrive.

Violet brought an amber necklace as her birthday present, and Barbara, dressed in her white party frock, with all traces of her tears removed, was prettily grateful for it.

"It's *charming*," she said, "and just what I wanted."

She had heard Aunt Olivia say that on her birthday, when grandfather had given her a little book-rest, and she had remembered it as a grown-up thing to say when people gave you presents.

As soon as all the guests had arrived, Jonathan came home from school, and, according to his mother's instructions, slipped upstairs to wash and change his suit before coming into the drawing-room. He washed and changed his suit, but he forgot to brush his hair, and came down with it sticking up in a wild semi-circle round his brows, where his washing operations had driven it. All Rachel's frenzied signs to him to go and brush it were lost upon him.

Dickie, yielding to the irresistible allure that Jonathan had for him, tried to make him talk of his exploits, and Jonathan, fully aware of the fascinated horror with which Dickie regarded him, was nothing loth. Swaggering, with hands in pockets, and long, thin legs planted well apart, a dare-devil smile on his keen, Puck's face, he retold his epic adventures of yesterday, exaggerating shamelessly, enjoying the horror that deepened every minute on Dickie's face. Dickie knew that he, himself, was wicked—he had stolen, and had nearly been sent to prison for breaking a window—but he didn't want to be wicked, and Jonathan did. He listened to Jonathan's account of the street fight, his eyes growing wider and wider. It was dreadful, it was wonderful, it was glorious. ... Next best to being good must be to be bad—gloriously, outrageously bad, like Jonathan.

As Jonathan swaggered, he was defying the secret feeling of loneliness that was always lying in wait for him, the feeling that nobody knew him and that he knew nobody.

"I'm not afraid of anything, or anyone, in the world," he shouted. And the little, mocking demon in his heart whispered, "You are, you daren't put your foot under a cart-wheel."

Clarissa arrived last of all, bringing a musical-box as her present to Barbara. When a spring was pressed, the lid opened, and a tiny bird shot up, opened its mouth, fluttered its feathered wings, sang for a minute or so, then went back into its box.

"But it's lovely," said Rachel.

"Daddy helped me choose it," said Clarissa shyly.

There was something delicate and ethereal about her that made every other child in the room seem suddenly clumsy and unattractive. She looked like a small pre-Raphael angel as she stood by Rachel, smiling her shy, sweet, serious smile.

"Isn't she a little beauty?" whispered Miss Nash to Olivia. "Her father's mad about her, you know. He can't bear her out of his sight."

"That's surely an exaggeration," said Olivia coldly, "considering that he's away at his office all day."

But, as she helped in the preparation of the games, she could not help watching Clarissa. The child was obviously unaware of her loveliness, ready always to efface herself. The thought of her being left to the doubtful mercy of Wanda, neglected, or, what would be worse, forced into Wanda's mould, was not a pleasant one. Wanda, of course, could not really hurt her while Stephen was there with healing for all her ills. There came into her mind the description of old Jolyon, in the *Forsyte Saga*, "His heart was made to be the plaything and beloved resort of tiny, helpless things." It might have been written of Stephen. Then she deliberately hardened her spirit. The child would soon adapt herself, soon forget Stephen, as Stephen would forget her.

Christopher arrived with a large doll just before tea. Barbara said that it was charming and just what she wanted, and Jonathan, who was now over-excited, claimed him as a fresh audience.

"And we fought and made them run away. . . . I *like* fighting."

"Yes, fighting's fun," said Christopher, "but you've got to learn how to do it."

"But I do know how to do it. I hit people and try to knock them down."

Christopher laughed.

"It's not as simple as that. Like everything else it's got to be learnt. . . . Look here, how would you like to have some boxing lessons?"

"*Oo!*" said Jonathan.

"I'll speak to your father and fix it up then," said Christopher, "and you'll soon find out that you can't fight as well as you think you can."

He left Jonathan testing the biceps of his puny arm, and seeing himself already a famous pugilist.

Barbara was being "bossy", but she was bossing kindly, and everyone was letting her have her own way because it was her party. Jonathan treated her indulgently, doing whatever she told him to, because he didn't want to spoil her birthday, but the knowledge that he could reduce her to tears, if he wanted to, by calling her "Jemima", was a secret source of pleasure to him.

"Doesn't she look *sweet*?" said Joy to Rachel, watching Barbara marshalling her guests. Rachel, touched by this, impulsively told Joy about Jonathan's escapade of yesterday. Ordinarily she took a good deal of pains to hide her children's naughtiness from Joy, convinced that news of the naughtiness of Jonathan and Barbara caused Joy to gloat triumphantly over the goodness of Dickie and Billy and Laura and Bobs. She had even warned Barbara to tell no one of Jonathan's street fight, especially Auntie Joy. But she enjoyed the confidence.

"I feel so ashamed," she ended. "What will people *think* of us?"

Then Joy, as impulsively, told Rachel about Dickie's stealing the toy monkey, and breaking the window—things that she had religiously hidden from her up to now.

Olivia and Violet were gathering the children together for another game, but Rachel and Joy still sat apart, enjoying the strange new intimacy that both were aware would vanish as suddenly and inexplicably as it had come.

"Olivia's losing her looks," said Rachel.

"Yes, isn't she?" agreed Joy. "I met her in the town yesterday and thought that she looked almost plain."

They spoke with a satisfaction that was as unconscious as was their occasional envy of Olivia, with her freedom from family cares.

"It's a funny thing," went on Joy, "but women with practically nothing to do seem to age more quickly than women who have to work hard."

"I wish I'd a little less to do," smiled Rachel.

"So do I. Children never give you a second's peace, do they?"

There was a placid superiority in their ruefulness. They were enclosed in the warm, happy fellowship of motherhood, while Olivia and Violet, for all their elegance, were outside in the cold.

Tea was a great success. The only contretemps was when Laura ate a piece of ginger-cake by mistake. Billy, however, rose to the occasion. He said, "If a dragon comes and eats you now, Laura, he'll find a piece of nasty cake inside you, and it'll burn his tongue, and you'll be glad."

The reflection afforded consolation and delight to Laura, and she began to chatter volubly to Christopher, who sat next to her. She said, "I can jump better'n' Bobs, an' run better'n' Bobs, an' talk better'n' Bobs, an' d'you know why? 'Cause I came here firster than Bobs."

Clarissa joined in the games with shy pleasure. She delighted in being among other children like this, especially if no one took any notice of her. She found Barbara's officiousness rather trying, but she loved Laura, and was storing up in her mind everything that she said, in order to tell Stephen afterwards.

In the babel at tea, while they were pulling crackers, Rachel suddenly relaxed. It was all right. The party was a success. She need not worry any more. All these children would take home enthusiastic accounts of it. Their parents would think well of her. They would ask Barbara and Jonathan back when they gave parties.

The Melliners became rather rough after tea, but Miss Nash, very bright, and worn, and tactful, managed to keep them within bounds. Joy was the first to go home. Bruce had got back early (it was one of Mr. Dawes' good days), and came to help her with the children. He carried Laura, Joy pushed the pram with Bobs, already half-asleep, and Miss Nash walked on ahead with the boys. Laura snuggled happily against Bruce's shoulder. She wasn't afraid of the man who killed little boys and girls for his shop window when Daddy was there. Only when it was Mummy, or Miss Nash. From the safe refuge of his shoulder, she gazed round-eyed at the lighted streets with the thick, dark shadows between the lamp posts. It was nearly the middle of the night. When it was quite the middle of the night, and everyone was asleep, the robbers would come out. Laura's mental picture of the streets at midnight was of a jostling throng of robbers completely filling them from pavement to pavement.

Just as Olivia was setting off, Stephen came for Clarissa, and they walked homeward together. A feeling of constraint that was almost guilt lay upon Olivia. It irked her pride, seemed to lay the smear of intrigue upon, her love, that they should have to pretend to be casual acquaintances before the child. Soon both of them fell silent.

Clarissa talked eagerly in her clear, high-pitched, childish voice, telling him about the party, how much Barbara had liked her musical-box, the funny things that Laura had said. . . .

When they came to the point where their ways parted, Stephen said: "May we see you home first?"

She said "No, but——" and looked around. Clarissa was standing some distance away making overtures to a cat that was rubbing itself round a lamp-post. Olivia spoke in a quick, low voice.

"Stephen, I must see you. When can you meet me?"

"Any time. Shall I come to your house?"

"No. Meet me in Henton Park again. At the Oak Tree."

"When?"

"To-morrow. At three o'clock."

Clarissa joined them.

"It was such a sweet one," she said, "and it felt thin. I'm sure it was hungry. It saw one of its friends and ran away."

"Good-bye."

Stephen's hand wrung hers painfully. Clarissa stood on tip-toe, and imprinted a soft kiss on her cheek.

As they disappeared Clarissa's sweet, excited voice floated back to her through the darkness.

It was a perfect November afternoon. The leafless hedgerows were gay with feathery tufts of old man's beard. In the distance the bare trees were etched against a primrose sky. The wood was a fairyland of gold and silver—filigree golden bracken standing waist high, golden beech leaves, gleaming silver birches, and over all a tracery of glistening hoar frost. Most of the leaves had fallen now, but some still clung to the trees.

He was at the seat waiting for her when she arrived. It was the first time she had seen him alone since her party.

"I had to talk to you, Stephen," she said. "It's Wanda. She knows."

He looked at her in surprise.

"I'm sure she doesn't."

"I'm sure she does."

"Why do you think so?"

"Something she said at my bridge drive."

"Wanda's always saying things that might mean anything."

"She meant this. She knows, and she meant me to know that she knows."

"She said nothing to me except"—— except her usual sneers, he meant. "In any case," he went on, "does it matter if she does know?"

"I suppose not," she said, slowly. "Only somehow it frightened me. I don't know why."

"Darling, why should it? We're waiting till the end of the month. I promised you that, though I'd like to have carried you off at once. And it may be sooner."

"It seems dreadful to be sitting and waiting for Derek's business to go smash."

"It was you who chose to do that."

"I know. . . . Stephen, answer me quite honestly. Do you feel any doubt?"

"You know I don't," he said vehemently.

"How should I know? It was all so sudden. It took us by surprise. We've had time to think it over in cold blood since."

"Too much time. It would have been better if you'd let me take you away then, as I wanted to."

"Perhaps it would. But it's too late for that now."

He looked down at her pale face.

"You mustn't let yourself get morbid," he said, gently. "It's all quite simple and straightforward. You love me, and I love you, and we're going away together as soon as it can be arranged. Think of it that way."

"Yes. . . . Stephen, you used to worry about Clarissa, and what would happen to her if you went away. Do you never worry about that now?"

She turned her face away suddenly, because she did not want to see his expression when he said "No."

Still looking away from him, she said slowly: "Then if it comes to choosing between Clarissa and me, which it does, I suppose, you choose me?"

His answer was to hold her closely to him. Clasped in his arms, her heart beating against his, her lips upon his, all the turmoil of her spirit died away. It was, as he had said, all quite simple and straightforward. He loved her, and she loved him. Soon—very soon now—this agony of waiting and of longing would be over.

They stood there in silence, as motionless as the trees around them, while the dead leaves fell slowly through the still air.

Chapter Twenty-One

DEREK MAINWARING was walking homeward, steering a zig-zag course as if he were drunk. The end had come at last. Fellows, his principal creditor, had told him that, if his account were not paid by the end of the week, he would issue a writ. Fellows had been patient, but his patience was exhausted at last. He had spoken bluntly, and rather contemptuously, telling Derek frankly that, since Sefton went, no one had felt the slightest confidence in his business. "A schoolboy with the most elementary knowledge of mathematics wouldn't have played the fool tricks you've played in the last few months."

The minute Fellows' writ was issued, the other creditors would close in on him. There would be a creditors' meeting, bankruptcy, a complete, inglorious smash. He had been to see his bank manager, and his bank manager had been as bluntly uncompromising as Fellows. The bank would not give him a penny's further credit. The manager had said that, unless he had taken for granted that the business would still be conducted on the lines on which Sefton had conducted it, he would not have given him what he had given him already.

Derek's mind darted to and fro like a rat in a trap. He heard again, in imagination, the easy sneers with which Ravenham would discuss the matter, and a cold sweat broke out all over his body. He stumbled into the house, and into the drawing-room, where Olivia sat by the fire with some household mending. The sight of her broke down the last vestige of his self-control, as the conviction came to him once more that somehow or other she must be responsible for all his troubles. He slammed the door and burst into a tirade of abuse. Literally beside himself, he poured out on her all the fury and anger and terror that was in his heart.

She raised her head with a sharp, startled movement at his abrupt entry. His eyes were bloodshot, and at first she thought he had been drinking, though that was a thing he seldom did. Then she sat quite motionless, listening to him, while the colour receded from her face, leaving even her lips white. He gave her no idea as to what had caused the outburst. He merely let flow a stream of venomous vituperation.

"You've been a millstone round my neck ever since I married you. Any other man would have got rid of you before now. What the hell use have you ever been to me? You couldn't even bear children!"

There was a sudden silence. The words shocked Derek and pulled him up short. He had not known that he was saying them. They came out at the bidding of the devil that possessed him, and knew what would hurt her most. He didn't mean them, as, indeed, he didn't mean any of his tirade. But he had said them, and he was not going to take them back. He stood glaring at her with bloodshot eyes. Why didn't she speak? Why didn't she say something? What was the matter with her? She looked as if she were carved in marble, sitting there staring in front of her. It seemed to him that the silence must last for ever, when suddenly it was broken by the ringing of the telephone bell. He stumbled out to the hall and took down the receiver. She heard him say surlily:

"Yes. Who is it?" Then eagerly, "Yes, I'll come at once."

Then she heard the slamming of the front door, and the house was silent again. She remained motionless, gazing in front of her, for some time, then she rose, folded her work, and put away her basket. That released her. She couldn't stay with Derek any longer after that. It released her from everything. She need not wait till the end of the month now. She need not wait till the state of his business declared itself. She need not wait another second.

She went to the telephone and rang up Stephen.

"I want you to come here. . . . Yes, at once. . . . I'll tell you when you come."

She put the receiver back, went upstairs to her bedroom, and packed her suit-case. She would just take things for the night. The others could be sent on after her. She had some good jewellery that her mother had left her; she would take that to sell. They must go away at once before to-night. Stephen could go home to pack his things, then meet her at the station. She hesitated as to whether to put on her hat and coat, and finally deciding not to. She could do that when Stephen had gone home to pack.

She heard a knock at the front door. . . . That must be Stephen. She fastened her suit-case, and went downstairs to the drawing-room, where he was waiting for her. He looked at her solicitously as she entered.

"You're ill, Olivia—you're——"

"I'm all right, I rang you up——"

"Yes, it was a queer thing, but I was just on the point of taking up the receiver to ring you up when your ring came."

"You wanted to speak to me?"

"Yes."

"What about?"

"Well. . . ." He looked slightly uncomfortable, then blurted out his story quickly, rather glibly, as if he had been rehearsing it in his mind. "I've been thinking about Clarissa. I don't know whether I ever told you, but I've got an uncle down in Surrey, who used to be very fond of me when I was a boy. He's got a son of his own, but he always had more in common with me. He was annoyed because I married Wanda without consulting him. He met her once, after the wedding, and didn't take to her, so dropped us both. He's got a rather decent place down in Surrey, and a lot of the big wigs in London go there for week-ends and things. Wanda was annoyed that he didn't take her up. . . . Well, I thought I'd go and see him and tell him exactly how things are. You see, if he'd have Wanda there occasionally, and let her meet the people who go there—they're the sort of people she's always wanted to meet—I thought that she might agree to let Clarissa go to stay with him sometimes, and then he could have us there when Clarissa's with him. He's a decent chap and not a bit strait-laced, and I'm sure Wanda would agree if she was getting something definite out of it. A sort of *quid pro quo*."

"I see."

She looked at him. He had forgotten her. His thoughts were with Clarissa—anxious, protective, guilty. She saw that look always between them in the years to come. He would never forget. He would always feel that he had deliberately abandoned Clarissa to unkindness and neglect. He would always blame himself. Perhaps he would even come to blame her. If she could have had children, he would have forgotten, but, as it was, he would never forget. He had known when he fell in love with her that she could not bear a child. He had said that it did not matter. But it did matter. . . . It would not have mattered with some men, but it would matter with Stephen. . . . He had not been quite honest with her about Clarissa, but that was because he had not been quite honest with himself. . . .

He roused himself from his abstraction.

"What was it you wanted to speak to me about?"

She was silent, bracing herself to her decision. Then, looking stonily in front of her, she said:

"Stephen, I can't come away with you. . . ."

"What do you mean?"

"What I said. It's all over. We shouldn't be happy."

He stared at her in blank amazement.

"Olivia, this is preposterous! After all you've said—after all the promises you've made me——"

"I know. I'm sorry. . . ."

"Darling," he said, gently, "tell me. What is it?"

"Just what I said. We shouldn't be happy."

"Do you mean you don't love me enough to take the risk?"

She was silent, then said:

"I suppose that's it."

He put his arm around her, but she broke jerkily away from his embrace.

"Please, Stephen. . . . I meant it."

He was hurt and outraged now.

"I can't understand you, Olivia."

"Don't try to. Just think me a fickle, changeable woman."

"You're the last woman in the world I expected this sort of thing from."

"It's as well you found out in time then, isn't it?"

She was hurting him deliberately. It was the only way. If she told him her real motive, he would protest and insist; he would persuade her against her reason, against her secret knowledge.

"Won't you tell me what's changed you?"

"It's what you said. I don't love you enough to take the risk."

He stood up. His lips were tightly set, the hollows in his cheeks deeply marked.

"It's—good-bye, then."

"Yes. Good-bye."

He turned abruptly on his heel and left her. She saw him walking down the garden path, his face pale and pinched. He was suffering, of course, but she wondered if there were already a faint relief in his heart.

She went upstairs and unpacked her bag, putting the things back carefully into their places. Then she went downstairs. She was thinking of the time they had stood in Henton Park wood, and she had said, "It would kill me to have to give you up."

Derek came home with a light, easy tread. All his fear and anger were gone. The Image was restored to its place. Sefton had restored it. . . .

It was Sefton who had rung him up asking him to meet him. At the end of their interview Sefton had entered the business again, not as manager, but as a partner, with an equal share in it.

Sefton had not been idle during these months since his dismissal. In returning to the business he could bring new and important customers to it; he could bring back old ones who had left it; he could lay his hands on enough ready money to pay off Fellows, and a few of the more pressing creditors. Since leaving it, he had kept his eyes on the progress of the business, and he had deliberately refrained from intervening till affairs were in such a state that Derek would accept his terms. He was a clever man, and had determined on this course within five minutes of his dismissal. He was ambitious, too, and intended now to work up the business for a few more years, and then buy Derek out. He had Derek well under his thumb, and expected little more trouble from him.

Derek was walking airily and smiling to himself. Sefton was a good chap, and he felt sincerely grateful to him. The disaster was averted by a fraction of an inch. He felt like a man condemned to be hanged, whose reprieve had arrived at the last minute. . . .

He held a large bunch of flowers in one hand, and a box of chocolates in the other. He had a vague, undefined feeling that he'd been a bit snappy with Olivia lately, and he wanted to make things all right again. After all, she was a good wife to him, and they were very fond of each other.

He did not acknowledge that he had actually been in the wrong with regard to her, because he never acknowledged that he had been in the wrong, but he did admit to himself that he might possibly have said some things that Olivia might possibly have misunderstood, and that was rather a lot for Derek to admit, even to himself.

The only thing in the whole world that Olivia wanted was to be left alone, and Derek would not leave her alone. He followed her up to her bedroom, laid the chocolates and flowers upon her dressing-table, and began fidgeting about. . . .

"I say," he said, "it's years since we went out shopping together. Let's go up to-morrow, and I'll get you something really swagger."

She did not know what he had said, but something automatically replied for her.

"Thank you. . . ."

He sat down on the edge of the bed and gave a short, embarrassed laugh.

"I daresay you've—thought me a bit—funny in my manner lately, old girl. I've had a few worries at the business. I haven't meant anything personal."

She was silent.

"I hope you didn't think that I meant anything personal," he said.

He was looking at her sheepishly—like a little boy, who had got into a temper, trying to tell her that he was sorry, but who was quite ready to fly into another if she rejected his overtures.

"When one's worried," he went on, "one doesn't quite think what one's saying."

He was so persistent that she had to gather together her scattered senses to attend to him.

"It's all right, Derek," she said steadily, "I know you've been worried."

He seemed relieved at the implied forgiveness.

"Every business has its ups and downs," he said casually, then, with a return to his manner of sheepishness. "If I have said anything that's seemed strange to you, you'll forget it, won't you? Honestly, I never meant anything personal."

Again she had to gather together her forces to attend to him."

"It's all right," she repeated, with a faint smile.

It occurred to her that, for the first time in their lives together, she felt to him just a little as Susan must have felt.

Chapter Twenty-Two

"I ASKED you to come," said Olivia, "because I wanted you to know that I'm not going away with Stephen after all. I decided yesterday."

Her tone was light, casual, almost gay. There were dark hollows and lines of strain beneath her eyes, but she had rouged and powdered carefully, her expression was composed, her head erect.

"Won't you tell me about it?" said Christopher gently.

She shrugged, and smiled again—a strained, schooled smile on lips whose limits of control were firmly fixed.

All through the long, hopeless night she had told herself: It will be better in the morning. But the morning had come and it was no better. She had sent for Christopher on an impulse of desperation that she was already regretting. She had thought: I must talk to someone about it, or I shall go mad. Now that he had come she found his sympathy, his solicitude, his almost womanly perception unendurable. He became an enemy, trying to break down the defences that she had so painfully raised.

"There's nothing to tell," she said lightly. "It's just that—I suppose we didn't love each other enough."

"It was the child?"

"Yes. If we'd loved each other enough, it would have made up for everything. Or, if I could have had a child——"

She jerked herself up, compressing her lips again into their strained smile. "I just wanted you to know, because you—understood."

She enunciated the words carefully, as if each one needed her whole attention. As she spoke, her eyes met his in a gaze that defied him to break down her composure. Her face was terrible in its youthlessness.

"It's all over?" he said.

"It's all over."

"There's no chance of your ever being happy with Derek?" he said timidly.

She shook her head.

"No, but there's no chance of my ever being as unhappy with him as I would have been with Stephen. You can't be hurt by someone you don't love."

He dared not offer sympathy in words, but the silence that followed was so pregnant with it that her tense frame suddenly quivered. She rose abruptly, still smiling her set, faint smile.

"You'd better go, Patrino. You understand too well."

"My dear," he said, "are you wise to take it like this?"

"How else could I take it?"

"Some women would——"

"Have a good cry and get it over? It sounds so simple, doesn't it? But tears don't really help, you know, Patrino."

"There's nothing I can do?"

"What could you do?"

He had wild ideas of going to Stephen, of going to Derek, of somehow forcing one of them to become the sort of man who would make her happy.

"Could I go to see Stephen?"

He realised, as he said it, how futile it sounded.

She shook her head.

"It's not just a misunderstanding, you know, Patrino. It's the end. Don't think that I'm ungrateful. You've been—terribly kind. But please go now."

There was a sudden urgency in her voice. He knew that she would never quite forgive herself or him if she broke down.

He turned uncertainly to the door.

"Don't come with me, my dear."

But she came, and stood at the front door till he had reached the gate. Then she waved, and called out "Good-bye," before she turned back into the house.

He carried away a poignant memory of her eyes ringed with

shadows, her face white and strained beneath its rouge, her lips set in that strained unhappy smile.

But, somehow, he felt less anxious about her than he had felt before. She was right. It hurt less to part from Stephen like this, than it would have hurt to watch his love for her slowly poisoned by remorse. This, for all the agony of it, was a clean cut. The other would have been a festering wound. By the time he reached home he was conscious almost of a sense of relief. The worst that he had imagined for her could never happen now. And time would dull the sharpness of her pain. She had the Gods' most precious gift of courage. There was something unconquerable about her.

He hung up his coat and hat in the hall, then stood irresolute outside his study door. He thought of the day when he had gone to see Olivia to ask if she knew anything about Susan and Charlie, and had found her more unhappy, more driven, more tormented than he was himself. Ever since then his anxious thoughts had been with her. Not once had they turned to Susan. But now, released from their long vigil with Olivia, they could turn again to Susan, and to their jealous agonised searching in the past. For a second he held them in check. He felt like a man driven by forces beyond his powers and understanding into a haunted room where some horror awaited him, like a child compelling himself against his will to look over his shoulder at a lurking bogey. Then, deliberately, he turned to face it. Susan ... Charlie. ...

"Did you never guess about Charlie and me?" He drew a deep, tremulous breath, and stood contemplating amazedly the incredible thing that had happened. He had entered the room to find it bright and wholesome, unhaunted by any terror. He had looked over his shoulder to find the bogey an empty imagining. Susan ... Charlie. ... "Did you never guess about Charlie and me?" The familiar expected anger failed to come. He felt no resentment, no jealousy. It had all died, consumed as it were in the flames of his pity for Olivia. He was conscious only of a peace so intense that it was almost ecstasy. It was as if Susan had come back to him after a long and wearisome absence. Suddenly he knew that it did not matter whether Charlie had been her lover or not. She had given him all he had needed of her. What he had had from her was his for ever—an imperishable possession. What he had not had could never have been his. The knowledge was a ray of warmth and light, flooding the dark bleakness of his spirit. A rush of passionate love for her, of joy at their reunion, swept over him. He flung open the drawing-room door, and entered it for the first time since his return from Cornwall. From the picture over the mantelpiece Susan smiled down at him. He stood on the hearthrug, looking up at it.

"I've been a fool, Susan," he said aloud. "Forgive me."

Chapter Twenty-Three

LYDIA put the last coffee cup on to her tray and went out of the room, closing the door behind her. There was a short silence. Then Joy said:

"It'll be Christmas in less than a fortnight now. . . . Shall we come here as usual, Father?"

"Of course," said Christopher, and added: "Is it as near as that?"

He was sitting in the leather arm-chair by his desk. Over the fire-place hung the portrait of Susan that used to hang in the drawing-room. It had been moved into his study that morning.

Already these Saturday evenings without Susan were beginning to seem normal and ordinary.

"Only one clear week before it," said Lethbridge, who was sitting in the arm-chair by the window smoking his pipe.

Lethbridge had retired from his practice now, and he and Christopher spent a good deal of their time together. He had been to the last two Saturday evening gatherings, and Christopher's children were glad to have him there. His presence, and the friendship it implied, took from Christopher a slight suggestion of pathos that he would otherwise have had, and relieved them of a sense of responsibility.

Christmas, of course, might be rather trying—the first Christmas without Susan.

"If you'd care to come to us?" said Joy vaguely.

"Oh, no, we'll have it here as usual," said Christopher. "Children are very conservative. Christmas wouldn't be Christmas to them if we had it in a different place, or played different games."

"Miss Nash and I will see to things," said Joy.

A short time ago Rachel would have felt that Joy was taking too much upon her, would even have suspected that Joy was deliberately planning to humiliate her, but now a strange serenity, that she had never known in her life before, lay like a spell upon her soul and body. Frank had laughed at her, and said that it was absurd of her to be sure so soon. But she was sure. This calm happiness, this radiant feeling of well-being could not mean anything else. She had not known it with the other two. She had felt frightened when Jonathan was coming, and when Barbara was coming she had felt resentful. She had never felt like this before, but still—she was sure. She had even stopped worrying about the other two. She laughed now at things in Jonathan that would have hurt her terribly a short time ago.

She heard Lethbridge asking Frank how Jonathan's foot was, and heard Frank answering:

"It's getting on very nicely. He's a careless little monkey. It wasn't the man's fault at all."

Coming home from school a week ago, Jonathan had had his foot run over by the wheel of a cart. He must, of course, have been walking in the road without looking where he was going. Someone had run to tell them what had happened, and Frank had gone to fetch him home at once. When he had arrived, his small face had been twisted with pain, and he was slightly light-headed. He must have been light-headed, because he kept saying exultantly, "I've done it—I've done it!"

The foot was badly crushed, but by a miracle no real harm was done, and he was already going about on crutches, on which he performed horrible acrobatic feats.

The accident had been a shock to her, but even through that her serenity had upheld her, and she had not "got into a state" about it, as once she would have done.

And the strange thing was that this new detachment from Jonathan seemed to have drawn him nearer her. Now that she was willing to say goodbye to the baby part of him, it was as if it had suddenly decided not to leave her. He would sit on her knee and kiss her, and, when she went to say good night to him, coax her to stay longer with him.

Joy's eyes were fixed on Bruce, as he sat talking to Christopher. He looked well and cheerful. She had known, as soon as he entered the house that afternoon, that it had been one of Dawes' good days. On Dawes' bad days, Bruce's face wore a peculiar grey tinge that nothing else ever brought to it.

Then her eyes went slowly to Olivia. Olivia had on a new, very smart dress of black satin that Derek had bought for her. Looking at her, Joy was conscious of that faint resentment that had never left her since her father had asked her to help Olivia, and she had refused. How absurd of him to have imagined that Olivia needed help. That dress had probably cost half what she, Joy, spent on clothes in a year. She had a better house than Joy's, and a more prosperous husband. She had everything she could possibly wish for.

"It'll suit him down to the ground," Lethbridge was saying: "He's always seemed more like a country-gentleman than a solicitor. He's got an aristocratic manner that will go with the job very well."

They were talking about Stephen Arnold. His uncle and cousin had been drowned yachting last month, and he had come into the property.

Olivia's eyes darkened as she listened, but she gave no other sign of emotion. They need not have worried about money, as things had turned out, but the real difficulty would have remained unsolved, unless, of course, Wanda had been open to a bribe. Still—it was no use thinking about it. It was all over and done with. She had not seen him since she had sent him away, but the knowledge that she might meet him whenever she went out had been like a precipice open always in front of her. Sometimes, when she approached the corner of a street, the thought that he might be coming to meet her only a few yards away, would set her heart racing, and make her knees so unsteady that she could hardly stand. Well, that was all over, too. He had left Ravenham. She need not be afraid of meeting him any more. . . .

Yesterday she had gone alone to the seat in the wood in order to try to break the spell of enchantment that the place had laid upon her thoughts. It had been dreary and desolate. The gold had fled, the trees were bare, the sodden beech leaves held a dull purplish tinge. A thin drizzle fell from the grey sky. She had fled from it in panic. It was ghost-ridden.

After her rupture with Stephen, she had seemed to those around her to grow gay and light-spirited. Derek had thought her more cheerful than he had known her for years, and had put it down to his tentative apology and carefully considerate treatment of her afterwards. (Women are quite easy to manage, he thought complacently, and she's awfully fond of me.) It was not all acting on her part. Utter hopelessness had brought to her a reckless desperation that produced the effect of light-heartedness.

That phase had lasted for a few weeks. Now she was growing quieter and more like her old self. Love had gone from her life for ever. She could never love Derek. However smooth their surface relations became, however well she learnt Susan's knack of managing him, she could never love him. To Susan he would always have been the first child she had carried beneath her heart. To Olivia he would always be an idol who had crumbled to dust before her eyes. And her love for Stephen was sick beyond hope of recovery. Her decision, and his acceptance of it, would always lie between them. She tried to steel herself to look forward without shrinking. Millions of women have to live without love. Something worth while could still be made of life. . . . She was gathering an armour of hope and courage around her, but any casual reference to Stephen still had power to pierce it.

Derek had gone across to Lethbridge, and was talking in his clear, pleasant voice:

"I'd given the old chap the sack, you know, and he was utterly down and out. Well, he crawled back, begging me to take him on again, and you'll never guess what I did. . . . I was a fool, of course, but it was one of those mad, impulsive things that I'm always doing. I said: 'All right, old man, I'll not only take you on, but I'll make you a partner.' I really think I only said it to see his face!

But, of course, I always stick to a thing I've said, so now the old chap's a partner, and still not quite sure whether he's awake or dreaming. I suppose that every old-fashioned business man would tell me I'm mad, but these flashes of imagination that I have generally justify themselves, and he's a man I can trust utterly to run the thing on my own lines. . . ."

Christopher listened to him with a smile. He had a pretty shrewd idea of the rights of the case. . . .

He looked round at the circle—Derek, Olivia, Joy, Bruce, Rachel, Frank—and remembered suddenly that evening, three months ago, when he had sat in this room with them, and they had seemed part of a dream, because he was tortured by jealousy of Charles Barrow. It was those weeks of torment that now seemed a dream.

There was a burst of conversation. Joy and Rachel and Olivia were talking about Jonathan's accident. Lethbridge and Frank were discussing an article in last week's *Lancet*. Derek was talking to Bruce about business methods, talking kindly and patronisingly as the head of a large business to an unimportant clerk.

To Christopher it was suddenly as if they were not there at all, as if he were alone in the room with Susan's portrait.

Her eyes smiled down on him, tender, understanding.

Milton Keynes UK
Ingram Content Group UK Ltd.
UKHW021616130524
442638UK00016B/72

9 781509 810291